Michael Underwood and The Murder Room

》》 This title is part of The Murder Room, our series dedicated to making available out-of-print or hard-to-find titles by classic crime writers.

Crime fiction has always held up a mirror to society. The Victorians were fascinated by sensational murder and the emerging science of detection; now we are obsessed with the forensic detail of violent death. And no other genre has so captivated and enthralled readers.

Vast troves of classic crime writing have for a long time been unavailable to all but the most dedicated frequenters of second-hand bookshops. The advent of digital publishing means that we are now able to bring you the backlists of a huge range of titles by classic and contemporary crime writers, some of which have been out of print for decades.

From the genteel amateur private eyes of the Golden Age and the femmes fatales of pulp fiction, to the morally ambiguous hard-boiled detectives of mid twentieth-century America and their descendants who walk our twenty-first century streets, The Murder Room has it all. 》》

The Murder Room
Where Criminal Minds Meet

themurderroom.com

Michael Underwood (1916–1992)

Michael Underwood (the pseudonym of John Michael Evelyn) was born in Worthing, Sussex and educated at Christ Church College, Oxford. He was called to the Bar in 1939 and served in the British army during World War Two. He returned to work in the Department of Public Prosecutions until his retirement in 1976, and wrote almost 50 crime novels informed by his career in the law. His five series characters include Sergeant Nick Atwell and lawyer Rosa Epton, of whom is was said by the *Washington Post* that she 'outdoes Perry Mason'.

The Crime of Colin Wise

Michael Underwood

An Orion book

Copyright © Isobel Mackenzie 1964

The right of Michael Underwood to be identified as the author of this work has been asserted in accordance with the Copyright, Designs and Patents Act 1988.

This edition published by
The Orion Publishing Group Ltd
Orion House
5 Upper St Martin's Lane
London WC2H 9EA

An Hachette UK company
A CIP catalogue record for this book is available from the British Library

ISBN 978 1 4719 0786 9

www.orionbooks.co.uk

For Yvonne Armstrong
who manages to decipher my handwriting

I

The young man held the small, pink oblong of paper lightly between his fingers and gazed at it with an expression of dreamy satisfaction. Then, folding it neatly across the centre and taking care that the two halves came exactly together, he slipped it into his wallet pocket with the same sure movement which had characterised its removal from the cheque-book.

He now picked the cheque-book off the desk and examined it intently. Satisfied that he had left no tell-tale mark to indicate that the topmost cheque and counterfoil had been extracted, he replaced the book in the drawer from which he had originally taken it. For the first time in five minutes he became aware of breathing again. He pocketed his penknife and then carefully gathered up the tiny fragments of debris which alone remained as evidence of what he had done. Kneading them together, he dropped the resulting pellet into an envelope, which he also put in his pocket.

His glance went quickly over the desk. He saw nothing, however, which could arouse the slightest suspicion and let out a soft sigh. Everything had gone with the precision of Swiss clockwork; so it needed to have done, considering the amount of thought and rehearsal which had led up to this moment.

Now, after weeks of preparation, the first overt act in his plan to grow rich had been accomplished.

He suddenly heard a movement in the next room and footsteps approaching the small study in which he was standing. Quickly he crossed over to the television set in the corner and was apparently busily engaged with a screw-driver when a voice caused him to look up.

"Still at it, Colin?"

1

Colin Wise smiled ruefully. "I've just about finished, Mr. Goodwin. I'm afraid you've had a lot of bother with this set, but I think it'll be all right now. I've fitted a new aerial lead plug." He straightened up. "Sometimes these sets seem to give nothing but trouble." He might have added, but didn't, that even the most reliable sets gave trouble when small faults had been deliberately created in order to ensure the necessity of further visits by the maintenance man. All that was now over, however, and for once the set really was in proper working order.

"If it packs up again, you can tell Mr. Gracey, I'll come and throw it right through his window."

Wise grinned. "It won't, Mr. Goodwin, don't worry. I've seen to that. It'll last till you go away and still be working when you come home in six months' time."

"You're staking your reputation high, aren't you?" Goodwin remarked with the familiar note of irony which Wise always found mildly disconcerting. As far as he could tell Goodwin had never begun to suspect the gentle sabotage of his television set and had completely accepted that it was the manufacturer's fault. From time to time, however, he was given to making remarks in a tone which caused Wise momentarily to wonder who was fooling whom. But he was never seriously concerned.

Wise looked about the room with a small, wistful smile. "I don't mind admitting, Mr. Goodwin, I shall miss coming here when you're away." There was almost a catch in his voice. "I've enjoyed my visits and appreciated your showing me all your things." He sighed. "One of the good points about this job is going into nice houses and meeting interesting people like yourself. In fact, you're the first author I've ever met."

"Most of them mend their own sets, I expect."

Wise brushed the flippancy aside. "I've always thought writing must be the nicest thing anyone could wish to do. I'd like to write a book myself one day." His expression became more melancholy. "But I haven't had the education."

"That's no bar these days. If you really want to write nothing'll stop you this side of cramp in the hand, but don't imagine it's all sunshine and sumptuous living. There are a great many easier ways of making money."

2

"You can say that again," Wise thought as he suppressed a desire to snigger.

"Anyway," Goodwin went on, "why am I addressing you like a writer's class, Colin? After all, you're an artist yourself. You know the pangs of creation."

Wise smiled modestly. "You *are* going to come in and see my drawings before you leave, aren't you? You said next Friday would suit you." With a new note of urgency he went on, "I very much want to show you round my small flat and hear how you think I've done it."

As Goodwin appeared to hesitate, Wise blurted out, "I shall be terribly disappointed if you don't come."

And more than disappointed too, he might have added. He had managed, however, to look so forlorn that Goodwin now said, "Yes, I'm sure I shall be able to manage Friday evening. I'm looking forward to it, too." He tapped his pocket. "Anyway, I have a note of it in my diary."

Wise breathed a silent sigh of relief. His whole careful plan hinged on Goodwin visiting his flat. He must come. He had to come. And Wise was ready to deploy every device of charm and persuasion he had in his armoury to make certain that he did come. Moreover, he was fundamentally confident that he would come. He had known that, as his day of departure drew nearer, Goodwin would inevitably become more preoccupied with the preparations necessary to a six-month sojourn in Australia; and the irony was, Wise could hardly counsel him to spare his energies or tell him that he wasn't going to get even as far as London Airport.

"What about a drink before you go?" Goodwin asked, turning back into the larger room.

"Thanks." Wise followed him through the connecting door.

"Vodka and tonic, is it?"

Wise nodded. "I've come to like vodka. It doesn't have such a taste of medicine as gin." He watched Goodwin busy himself at the small mahogany cabinet which had been converted into an unobtrusive drink cupboard. Like the study which they had just left, the present room had an air of lived-in comfort. The two heavy wing chairs, the deep sofa, the fitted carpet of dull gold, and the four pictures which hung on two of the walls, all testified to the quiet taste of their owner. Wise strolled over and stood in front of one of the pictures.

"You like my Jamini Roy, don't you?" Goodwin remarked, handing him his drink. "If I come back through India I'm going to see if I can pick up another."

"I like it very much," Wise said in a slowly thoughtful tone.

"Shall I tell you why?"

"Why?"

"It combines earthy sturdiness with just the right amount of artistic imagination." Goodwin's eyes glinted with amusement as he spoke.

"Is that it?"

"You tell me."

Wise moved forward a step and examined the picture more closely. "I think you're right. I think that may be why I do like it." He turned to Goodwin. "But what made you say that?"

Goodwin laughed. "Simply, because it's the reason I find it an appealing picture. I wasn't meaning to insult your artistic judgment." He held up his glass. "Cheers, Colin."

"Cheers, Mr. Goodwin, and I hope you have a successful trip."

"Thanks."

"Will you do much writing while you're away?"

"A few articles perhaps. And I shall try and work out the plot for a new novel which I want to write when I arrive back. I don't actually have much time to write while I'm out there. It's largely taken up with business. An uncle left me a couple of farms a few years ago, one in New South Wales, one in Queensland. They're pretty sizeable by English standards, and there's usually quite a lot to attend to even though I do have competent agents on the spot."

Colin Wise listened in polite interest, taking occasional sips at his drink, and reflecting that Goodwin would have been disagreeably surprised to learn just how much he already knew about those Australian farms. His almost weekly visits to tend the permanently ailing T.V. set had enabled him to familiarise himself with the most intimate details of Goodwin's affairs. He knew, for instance, that the farms had recently been valued at over fifty thousand pounds each. He also knew that Goodwin's investments in this country amounted to a further seventy thousand.

No wonder Goodwin had just now said there were easier ways of making money than by writing. *He* should know.

Wise regathered his thoughts as Goodwin went on to give a humorous description of life on an Australian farm and fell to a covert study of his intended victim. He reckoned he was around twice his own age, say forty-six. Curiously enough, his age was one of the few personal details Wise had not uncovered, not that it was of any consequence. He was broad-shouldered, had more than the beginnings of a tummy, and was fighting a losing battle to retain his hair-line. One detail Wise had not been able to make up his mind about was whether or not his teeth were his own. He would doubtless discover that in due course, not that it mattered either.

Goodwin was an amusing talker, and as Wise listened his attention turned to a study of his own reflection in the full-length mirror which covered the wall opposite the window and which helped to light the low-ceilinged room. What he saw was a slim young man of about five feet eight inches, with a close crop of dark hair and a pair of sad eyes set in a sallow face whose skin always looked smooth and well shaved. The mouth was firm and, like his other features, fitted his face to make it a deceptively agreeable mask for the coldly determined mind which lay behind.

Goodwin reached the end of his tale with an anecdote about the odd sexual behaviour of a kangaroo, and Wise's expression crinkled to register amusement. He drained his glass.

"I must be going, Mr. Goodwin, or I'll have Mr. Gracey on my tail. He wouldn't approve of my fraternising with the customers."

"You'd better tell him to send me a bill within the next few days or he won't get his money."

"I'll do that." Wise moved across to the door. "See you on Friday evening then, Mr. Goodwin. About half-past eight if that's convenient? You've got my address, haven't you?"

5

"Yes, *and* the directions you gave me," Goodwin replied blithely.

Wise let himself out of the cottage and strode down the short, narrow path to the pea-green van standing in the road outside which bore on its sides the legend: J. GRACEY, Radio and Television Specialists and Engineers, 246 Canal Street, Uxbridge, Middlesex.

As he switched on the ignition, he turned and gave the cottage the sort of appraising look it might have received from a prospective purchaser. He liked it—liked it very much—but there was no point in wasting time on daydreams. It was out of the question that he could ever settle there, but it should fetch a nice price, and that was going to be to his benefit if everything went as planned.

With a gesture of impatience at his own thoughts, he thrust the van into gear and surged away from the gate. The clock on Fulmer church said a quarter to one as he drove through the village in the direction of the main London-Oxford road. He had no more calls to make until mid-afternoon, and had told Mr. Gracey he expected to be back in the shop soon after midday. Now he couldn't make it before one o'clock, which meant two o'clock, since the shop always closed during that hour. Mr. Gracey would grumble, of course, but he wasn't a bad old stick at heart, and for the most part he and Wise conducted a relationship bred of self-interested mutual toleration.

Half-way down Denham Hill, Wise pulled off the road and unwrapped the fried-egg sandwich which he made for his lunch each day and which was followed always by an apple. His meal finished, he pulled a copy of an Ian Fleming paperback from the door pocket and settled himself diagonally across the front of the van to read for half an hour.

But for once he failed to get caught up by the story, and after starting the same sentence three times and breaking off to stare abstractedly through the windscreen, he put the book down and surrendered his mind to its own thoughts. He felt for the cheque and gingerly extracted it from its warm hiding-place. As pink and as fresh as a dog's tongue, he thought, putting it away again. Today was Monday. He'd fill in the details when he reached home this evening and post it to the bank so that it would arrive tomorrow morning. He had already drafted a letter addressed to Goodwin's own bank on Goodwin's own writing-paper saying that the cheque drawn in favour of Mr. Peter Fox was in order and could be properly cleared.

Peter Fox! William Carter! He grinned as he contemplated the bank accounts in these two names which he had been quietly operating over the past six weeks in preparation for present events.

For a long time he had not seen how he could possibly convert the forged cheque to his own profit without danger of discovery. Then the solution had suddenly come to him. He must open not one but two false bank accounts. Hence tomorrow Peter Fox's account at the Shepherd's Bush branch of the United Bank would be credited with a cheque for six thousand pounds drawn on Geoffrey Goodwin's account. Two days later Mr. Fox, a young man who bore no superficial resemblance to Colin Wise, would draw out six thousand pounds in cash, and on that same day Mr. William Carter would pay this very considerable sum into his account with the Earl's Court branch of the Southern Bank.

Wise had been gratified by the relative ease with which he had been able to open the false accounts. In each case a couple of forged references and a bit of form filling had been all that was required. It had been quite simple to one who was prepared to think out every detail before making a move. But then, if you were proposing to murder someone, nothing could be left to chance, or as near nothing as possible.

In Wise's case the commission of the murder was in itself a measure of security, a logical sequence in the concealment of the forgery and, if all went well, the key which would open the door to Goodwin's entire estate. For in the course of his numerous visits to the cottage he had been through all of Goodwin's business papers he could find and made careful notes of such items as his lists of investments and the whereabouts of share certificates and title deeds. A trip to Australia might eventually be necessary to shake the ripest fruit off the tree, and he rather fancied the idea. Wasn't this the pattern of murder committed by Haigh? Except, of course, that in the end he had paid the price of carelessness. And Wise didn't intend to be careless. He remembered reading all about the Haigh case when he'd been a small boy at school in Somerset, and he wondered what the villagers of Farthingmoor would think if they knew that the Colin Wise who had grown up in their midst was embarking on a life of single-handed crime of prodigious dimensions.

One family who would not evince surprise, or at least pretend not to do so, would be the Pritchards, he reflected grimly, for Mr. and Mrs. Pritchard (Uncle Tom and Aunt Joyce) had been his foster-parents and after seventeen years had had few illusions left. He could picture them at this moment sitting in their barn-like kitchen digging into enormous platefuls of steaming food, each far too occupied to talk—Uncle Tom with his hair mussed up at the back and a livid mark across his forehead where his cap had pressed. Aunt Joyce would be in one of her flowered pina-fores, her hair parted in the middle and pulled back into a bun, which looked like a pin-cushion, it was stuffed with so much metal. Her jaws would be clicking rhythmically as she tackled her food with stolid determination. But most of all he re-membered her moustache, its short black hairs emphasising the corners of her disapproving mouth. How, as a small boy, he had been fascinated and repelled by that moustache!

He remembered as if it were yesterday the first time he had looked up from his own plate one supper-time and asked, "Why do I call you Uncle Tom and Aunt Joyce and not Mummy and Daddy?" It had seemed a perfectly sensible question at the time.

"Because we're not your real father and mother," Aunt Joyce had replied, the corners of her mouth turning abruptly down farther.

"Where are my real father and mother?"

"I don't know."

"But they must be somewhere?"

"Get on with your food, Colin, and don't ask so many questions."

"Do you know where they are, Uncle Tom?"

"Do as Aunt Joyce says and get on with your food."

A few days later "The lady", as he always thought of her, called at the farm. It was only later that he learnt she came from the County Council Children's Department. He had, however, viewed her with scorn ever since she had come round a corner of a building and let out a small shriek on finding him wringing the neck of a hen. When she had remonstrated with him he had described to her with unconscious relish how he set about killing rabbits. He couldn't understand what all her fuss was about. She doubtless ate chicken and rabbit and must know that some-one had to kill the creatures. What was wrong with his acting as executioner, particularly as the rôle aroused no emotions in him?

As she was about to leave on this particular occasion she said to him, "You like being with Uncle Tom and Aunt Joyce, don't you?" He had made no reply, and she had continued, "Your real mother and father went away, that's why Uncle Tom and Aunt Joyce look after you."

"Where did they go?"

"I can't tell you, dear. I'm afraid they just went away and left you when you were a tiny baby."

It was only years later that he learnt that no one could tell him who his father was, since not even his mother had known. And she had disappeared within a few weeks of his birth and not since been heard of. It was at the same time as he became aware that the Pritchards were paid to bring him up.

Looking back now, he didn't pretend that his upbringing was responsible for turning him into a criminal. It was, he reckoned, largely a matter of temperament, and that was something with which you were endowed at birth. So, more likely than not he'd have turned to crime, anyway. Self-pity, the common motive force with most criminals, never occurred to him. At school he had been a self-contained boy who had despised the soft centres and crumbly corners of the other children long before he'd become properly aware of his own antecedents. All that he did admit to himself was that his background had conveniently divested him of any obligation toward society. His creed was every man for himself and survival of the fittest. He didn't even pretend that Aunt Joyce's lack of maternal warmth or the occasional beatings administered by Uncle Tom had warped him. And proof of this, and that he didn't consider he had been

9

ill-treated by his foster-parents, lay in the fact that he remained in their home as a lodger after he had left school and while he was learning a trade. It hadn't been until *he* was ready to leave that he had made his departure, and then he had done so finally, completely and without prior notice. That had been six years ago, and during that time he had not sent them so much as a Christmas card.

He liked to regard these last six years as a period of patient preparation for the moment of fulfilment which was now at hand. He didn't regret the time he had spent looking around to decide how he could most easily achieve his life's aim which, quite simply, was MONEY. Money with which to indulge his expensive and curiously fastidious tastes. Grandiose schemes required careful planning—the more so when they represented a one-man enterprise. It gave him a sense of glowing satisfaction as he now sat in the van beside the busy main road to reflect that there was not one single person in the whole wide world who had an inkling of what lay darkly in his mind.

He released the handbrake and steered the van back on to the road, allowing it to free-wheel to the bottom of the hill before starting the engine. A quarter of an hour later he pulled into the yard behind Mr. Gracey's shop and got out. He entered by the back door which led direct into the small office behind the shop.

Mrs. Gracey, a fading blonde of around forty, was bent over a catalogue. A cigarette jutted from the corner of her mouth, and her shoulders were hunched beneath one of the thick home-knitted cardigans she invariably wore regardless of temperature. This one was apricot yellow and utterly unbecoming. Colin Wise had never known a woman who so persistently wore the wrong colours.

He poked his head through the curtained doorway which led into the shop and saw that it was empty. It sometimes happened that customers would cough and scrape their feet until their throats were sore and their shoes worn through without Mrs. Gracey hearing them. She wasn't deaf, just endlessly preoccupied.

"Mr. Gracey in the workshop?" he asked.

"He was expecting you back before now," she replied, without looking up from her catalogue.

"The job at Mr. Goodwin's took longer than I'd expected."

"Then we must charge him a bit more," she said in a satisfied tone.

"Incidentally, he's going away at the end of this week and asked me to say that if you wanted to be paid before he left you'd better send in the account immediately." He pulled a piece of paper out of his pocket. "Here's a note of the work I did today."

She peered at it through eyes half closed against the smoke from her cigarette. "I'll put his account in the post tonight," she said, sticking the piece of paper beneath one of several used cups in her vicinity. "Where are you calling this afternoon?"

"Miss Comber's."

She turned her attention to the well-thumbed desk diary. "The picture jiggles about and people become strange shapes," she read out.

Wise grimaced. Poor (cloying) Miss Comber, she did seem unduly accident prone in regard to television sets. One had actually gone in for spontaneous combustion. But she was a soft-hearted old girl who had taken a considerable fancy to him.

Leaving Mrs. Gracey lighting a fresh cigarette from the butt of the other, he made his way across the yard to the workshop.

"Oh, you're back at last!" Mr. Gracey greeted him before he had time to close the door.

"The job at Mr. Goodwin's took longer than I'd expected," he repeated mildly.

"I've noticed the jobs at the posh houses always do take you longer." Wise assumed an expression of untroubled innocence, and Mr. Gracey went on, "You rather fancy yourself in those places, don't you?"

Wise gave a slight shrug. "I don't know about fancying myself. It's interesting to see how the other half of the world lives."

Mr. Gracey snorted. "Doesn't do any good getting ideas above your station. You'll never belong with them."

"That's just where you're so wrong, my friend," Wise thought grimly. Aloud he said, "I'm not getting ideas above my station, but this job'd be flaming dreary if one went only to houses like Miss Comber's."

"What's wrong with it? She's rich, that old girl."

"I know she is, but that doesn't prevent her house being as inviting as a railway waiting-room."

Mr. Gracey gave another snort. For one who couldn't tell beef from mutton, and furthermore didn't care, he could hardly be expected to be sympathetic towards his employee's interest in other people's homes.

"Well, now that you are back you can come and give me a hand over here."

The bench at which they worked was littered with pieces of dismantled sets, whose owners would surely have been filled with doubt and dismay had they been able to see what went on.

Mr. Gracey, who was short and fat and chronically short of breath, became redder and redder in the face as he bent to their task. Occasionally a particular piece of exertion brought forth a muttered oath, for he had no special aptitude for his trade, and Wise often wondered why he hadn't chosen to do something in which fingers played a less important part. Mr. Gracey's were like sausages—not chippolatas either—and he was forever scattering small parts about him or groping fiercely for an invisible screw. Wise, who had been in his employ for nearly twelve months, had no illusions about his value to the business. Mr. Gracey would be lost without a capable assistant and, recognising this fact, paid accordingly. Well, the time was not far off when he would have to be searching for a fresh assistant, and Colin Wise didn't care whether he found one or not. *He* had no intention of calling on Mr. Gracey's service when his own set broke down.

"I'd better be getting along to Miss Comber's," he said, as Mr. Gracey retrieved a final screw from the floor. At the door he paused. "Would it be all right for me to borrow the van on Friday evening? I have to go and fetch a chair I've bought in a sale. I'll pay, of course, for the petrol I use."

"I don't know why you don't buy a car of your own. I pay you enough," Mr. Gracey observed sourly.

"It'll be all right, then?"

"Suppose so. Mind you have it back here first thing on Saturday morning, though."

"I will. Thanks, Mr. Gracey."

He walked over to the van and was about to get in when he stopped. "What are you doing here, Lesley?"

Lesley Gracey, sixteen and not unattractive, was sitting in the passenger seat. Her awareness of her appeal to the opposite sex made it doubly frustrating that the one man whom she wished to impress appeared impervious to her charms. But the fact was that Colin Wise eschewed emotional entanglements: they had no part in his plan, and he had no wish to become the focal point of anyone's affection.

If Lesley Gracey had happened to drift his way as a casual pick-up, he'd have been ready to have passed a few lustful hours in her company; but since it hadn't worked like this, no other relationship was possible so far as he was concerned. The semiregular demands of his sexual appetite were met by a visit to the West End. The body's needs were catered for, the heart was never involved.

"I thought I'd come in the van with you to Miss Comber's," she said, her eyes roaming hopefully over his face.

"You know your father doesn't like your coming out in the van."

"But you don't mind, do you?"

"That has nothing to do with it. I just don't want to get the sack, and I might do if he sees you. He'd blame me."

"I'd tell him it was my idea."

Wise sighed. Her attentions were becoming a nuisance. She was constantly waylaying him and trying to excite his interest.

"Out, Lesley, there's a good girl."

While she appeared to be deliberating the situation, he leant across her to open the door. As he did so, she seized his hand and rubbed it against her cheek. "You haven't yet invited me to your flat and you promised you would."

"I will."

"When? Why not this week?"

"No, not this week."

"Next week then."

"Perhaps if you do as I ask now."

But she showed no signs of moving. "Have you had many girls up there?"

"No."

"I'm glad. Shall I be the first?"

"I can't remember."

"What day next week?"

"I haven't definitely promised that it will be next week. It depends."

"You're always finding excuses to put me off," she said, pouting her lower lip. Her expression brightened. "I might just drop in to see you."

"You mustn't," he said in a shocked voice.

"Why not? Have you something to hide? I believe you have—you're blushing."

"I'm not and I haven't." He gave her a shy smile and his tone became cajoling. "It's just that when you do come I want to have everything nicely prepared for your visit."

"All right," she said, apparently mollified and making a move towards getting out of the van. "What time will you be back?"

"In about an hour, I expect."

"I shan't be here then. I have to go and do my homework. Shall I see you tomorrow?"

"I'll be in and out." He started up the engine and slipped into gear.

"'Bye, Colin," she called out eagerly, as he made a sweeping circle to drive out of the yard. She gave him a wave, which he returned.

A minute later he had forgotten her; nor was he thinking about Miss Comber and her jiggling picture. His mind dwelt entirely on the sequence of events he had set in train and now not far off their climax.

His hand, like a homing pigeon, moved to his wallet pocket. The cheque was still snugly there.

2

As the lights turned red Wise jumped off the bus, bought an evening paper from the vendor on the corner and turned with brisk, purposeful steps down the road which led to his home. There were not many people about, and he took no notice of the few who did pass him in the dusk.

The large Victorian houses on either side, each standing in its own over-grown garden, provided little sign of life either. Several of them, he knew, were empty and awaiting the demolition squad, followed by the acquisitive descent of a speculative builder. But by that time he'd have gone and they could do what they liked. Meanwhile, however, he relished the atmosphere of seedy decay which formed a sort of cordon sanitaire around his home.

At the bottom of the road he passed through a pair of high wooden gates and stepped into a small yard. His yard. Making sure that the gates were properly closed behind him, he pulled out his key and opened the bright-red front door, from which a flight of stairs ascended steeply. It was an old coach-house, the only surviving portion of a property which had been pulled down several years before and replaced by a block of offices which bounded a road on the farther side.

To Colin Wise it was an oasis, and each evening he experienced the same glow of warm contentment as he mounted the stairs. This was his home, the first proper home he'd ever had. Furthermore, its atmosphere of welcome had been of his own making. The whole place had been in a state of advanced dilapidation when he'd acquired the lease eighteen months before. Now, thanks almost entirely to his own efforts, it had been transformed into a home anyone would be pleased to live in. And for Colin

Wise the absence of wife, dog, cat or even canary in no way diminished the sense of welcome he felt extended towards him by its walls.

He went first into his bedroom and changed out of the jeans and windcheater he wore for work and put on a pair of fawn slacks and a thick, charcoal-grey cardigan with a high collar. Though small, his bedroom represented to him the highest attainable in comfort. It was wall-to-wall carpeted—not very good quality carpet, maybe, but the best he could afford. The divan bed was luxurious after most of the ones he'd slept in, and a bedside lamp provided the only lighting in the room. The walls were honey-coloured and bare, apart from one of his own pen-and-ink sketches showing a corner of Lincoln's Inn Fields which had taken his fancy.

He hung his working clothes up in the cupboard, removed the cover from his bed, which he was scrupulous about making before leaving the flat in the morning, and went into the kitchen.

First he helped himself to a bottle of lager from the small refrigerator, then set about preparing his evening meal. He enjoyed cooking, and never had the bachelor's normal inclination to feed out of tins. While the steak was grilling, he mixed a salad and made the dressing. When all was ready and he had laid a place at the table, he lit a cigarette and, leaning against the sink, scanned the evening paper, which he continued to read as he ate. His meal over, he washed-up and put everything away. He couldn't bear dirty dishes lying about longer than necessary, and made almost a fetish of emptying ash-trays.

At length he was ready to get down to the business of the evening. Fetching the cheque, he seated himself at his living-room desk and for a few seconds stared at it with concentrated thought. Then he reached for a sheet of foolscap, and in the hand which he had practised to near perfection in the past few weeks he wrote first "Peter Fox", then "Six thousand pounds", followed by the same amount in figures. He had also noticed that Goodwin inserted the date in figures on his cheques. Finally, holding the pen a little tighter, his tongue creeping out of the corner of his mouth with concentration, he bent over the piece of paper and, making a sudden dart at it, rapidly signed the name

"Geoffrey Goodwin" six times before pausing to study his handi-work. Yes, they were pretty fair specimens; each good enough, he reckoned, to pass the eye of an unsuspecting bank clerk.

Like a tennis player warmed by a knock-up, he was now ready to begin. Placing the cheque in front of him, he took a deep breath, and in one non-stop movement filled in the particulars. Only when he had completed the signature did he sit back and examine the result. It was as good as he could have made it.

After this it was child's play. First he drafted a letter to his own bank or rather to Peter Fox's bank.

"Dear Sir," it read, "Please credit my account with the en-closed cheque for £6,000. Yours faithfully, Peter Fox."

Next he read over the letter which he had typed a few days earlier and signed in Goodwin's name.

"Dear Sir," this one ran, "I write to inform you that I have drawn a cheque for £6,000 in favour of Mr. Peter Fox and that this may be met without further reference to me. I am writing this letter as I am going abroad in a few days' time and don't wish there to be any hold-up in the matter. I require no acknowledge-ment of this letter. Yours truly, Geoffrey Goodwin."

Wise had remembered that Goodwin was always "Yours truly" to his bank manager.

He sealed the two envelopes with extra care and set off for the post. As he walked back along the quiet street his thoughts dwelt on the items he was proposing to buy with his six thousand pounds.

Ever since he'd been a small boy he had determined that he would one day become the owner of a motor-car. Not just any old car such as clogged the roads every day, but a real car. A car of aesthetic design, of handmade finish, of exhilarating speed—a panther amongst cars. And until he could afford such a car he preferred to be without, scorning to be the owner of any ordinary mongrel make. Now he'd be able to pore over the beautifully coloured brochures to practical purpose.

And after a motor-car, a fine picture, followed by the trappings of a luxurious home. These were the items for his money. The first six thousand, however, wouldn't stretch beyond a car

17

and a picture. The trappings must wait, but not for long, he hoped.

He had visited most of the private galleries in London and had decided that pride of ownership would be served by a French impressionist. A Cezanne perhaps, or a Dufy. Not a Renoir. He'd like to have a Gauguin some day, but for once even he was deterred by the price.

He smiled to himself. It was an unusual shopping list, but then he was an unusual person.

He turned into the main road, and a few minutes later arrived outside the post office. It was ten minutes past eight. His two letters would just catch the last collection. The day's plans had gone without a hitch.

He felt tired and exhilarated at the same time, and knew that if he returned home now he would only prowl around restlessly until he went to bed. He experienced what for him was rare indeed, a yearning for human company, and decided to visit his friend Patrick Fox.

Some people are given to referring in proprietary tones to "my friend" when they really mean "one of my friends". But in Colin Wise's case "my friend" was strictly apposite since the old man was the only person with whom he would claim any degree of friendship.

On the face of it they were as different as two males could be, and, in addition, Patrick Fox was old enough to be Wise's grandfather. But the bond which joined them together was the respect each had for the other's almost arrogant spirit of independence. Wise had first met Fox some months before when he had called at the old man's house to mend his radio. The set, which was antiquated, had in fact been beyond repair, and Wise had subsequently made him one out of cannibalised parts when Mr. Gracey wasn't looking. Since then he had been accustomed to call in from time to time and chat with the old man.

He arrived at the end house in a row of small villas and knocked. A second or two later he heard the tap of the old man's stick as he came along the passage. The door opened.

"'Evening, Patrick."

"Oh, it's you, Peter boy. Come on in."

"*I'll* shut the door," Wise said, stepping inside.

Fox turned and, using his white cane like an antenna, led the way into his back parlour. Wise never ceased to admire the brisk, sure fashion in which the old man moved about. God grant, however, that he might never become blind.

"Postman not left anything recently?" he asked, sitting down opposite Fox.

"Expecting a letter, were you, Peter boy?"

"Not really, though there'll probably be one for me from my bank in the next couple of days."

"Your bank! You're the only Fox I know, Peter boy, who's got a bank account. It proves we can't be related." He chuckled and looked in Wise's direction with grey, sightless eyes. "Going to read me the evening paper now you are here?"

"Sure, I've brought it with me," Wise replied, pulling the folded newspaper from his pocket. "Radio working all right?"

"Battery's running a bit low, I think."

"I'll bring along another next time I come."

"I'd like to repay you one day, Peter boy, but——"

"No repayment's necessary," Wise broke in with some embarrassment.

"I've never said this before, but I sometimes wonder why you bother with me." There followed a full minute of silence. "O.K., Peter boy, I don't want you to answer. I shouldn't have said that. It's good enough that you come and see me. People like you and me don't need to go behind the scenes. We can be friends without that." He had continued to stare in Wise's direction as the words tumbled out. He now sat back in his chair slightly out of breath and rested his hands on his thighs.

"Shall I start, Patrick?" Wise asked quietly.

"Yes, read to me, Peter boy."

For the next twenty minutes Wise read out bits and pieces which he thought would interest the blind man. When he had finished they embarked on a spirited discussion of the care of old people, which had been an item in the paper.

"Time I went home, Patrick," he said, when they'd exhausted the subject. "Anything else I can do before I go?"

"Nothing, Peter boy."

They bade each other good night and Wise departed. Fox never asked him when his next visit would be, and Wise similarly refrained from making a specific arrangement. This, each knew, was a proper reflection of their relationship.

On the first few occasions that they had met Fox hadn't even bothered to ask him his name, and by the time he came round to it Wise had realised that it would suit him to provide the blind man's address in connection with one of his false bank accounts. And if his address, why not adopt his name as well, even to the same initial. So when Patrick Fox had one day inquired after his name, Wise had replied with a laugh, "Same as yours. Fox. Peter Fox."

Wise had only had to mention that he didn't trust the landlady in his supposed digs for Fox to agree readily to his having mail addressed to his home. So far there'd been none, but it now seemed probable that the Shepherd's Bush branch of the United Bank, which carried Peter Fox's account, would shortly be acknowledging receipt of a cheque for six thousand pounds.

Wise had never had any qualms about his deception of the blind man. It was harmless and didn't affect the genuine regard in which he held him. Indeed, in one sense it might be seen as the repayment of what Wise did for him. Yes, that was the right way of looking at it, Wise reflected as he strode home.

As he switched out his bedroom light and snuggled down into the womblike warmth of his bed, he felt that no one could ever have embarked on murder with such unruffled efficiency and thoroughness.

There was a smile of simple innocence on his lips as he drifted into sleep.

3

The next day, Tuesday, and Wednesday passed off without event. Wise was out on deliveries and repairs the greater part of each day and was mostly able to keep out of Mr. Gracey's way. Lesley Gracey ambushed him in the yard on Wednesday afternoon and again tried to extract from him a firm invitation to his flat. He had recourse to further evasion, and their short encounter ended on an uncomfortable note. He decided with considerably mixed feelings that he had better make her a peace offering as soon as possible. Chocolates would do, though he also realised that she was likely to construe such an act as a symbol of burgeoning affection. There were dangers either way, but the greater ones seemed to lie at the moment in trying to freeze her off. There was more than a smear of her father's obstinacy in her make-up.

On Wednesday night he called round to see Patrick Fox, and there, sure enough, was a letter waiting for him from the United Bank saying that the cheque for six thousand pounds had been received to the credit of Mr. Peter Fox's account.

About eleven o'clock on Thursday morning he entered a public call box near Uxbridge Station and telephoned the bank.

"This is Mr. Peter Fox speaking," he announced to the girl who answered. "I shall be coming in around one o'clock to cash a cheque . . . er . . . rather a large one, so I thought I'd better let you know."

"How much will you be drawing, Mr. Fox?" the girl asked crisply.

"Six thousand pounds."

"I see. We'll have the money waiting for you now we know. How would you like it?"

"Fivers will do."

21

"That'll be all right, Mr. Fox. Thank you for ringing."

It was ten minutes past eleven when he stepped out of the box, which gave him approximately one hour to complete his next two jobs.

Shortly after noon he parked the van outside his home and dashed in to change into a suit. Minutes later he emerged bearing an empty holdall, a raincoat, a furry green hat and a pair of hornrimmed spectacles with lenses of plain glass. It took him no more than twenty minutes to reach Shepherd's Bush, where he parked the van down a side road. There he assumed his simple but effective disguise and strode purposefully towards the bank.

It was almost empty and only two tellers were on front counter duty. He approached the nearer one, who was counting a cascade of loose coins.

The clerk looked up with a raised eyebrow as he still went on counting. Wise took out his wallet, extracted the cheque which he had completed in advance and pushed it across the counter.

"Oh yes, you phoned earlier, Mr. Fox." Wise nodded. "We have the money ready for you. Do you wish to check it?"

Wise shook his head and smiled faintly. "No, I trust you."

The clerk seemed relieved. "Have you something to carry it in?"

"This. Is it big enough?" He passed over the holdall.

"Yes, this'll do. These," the clerk said, producing a wad of five-pound notes, "are in bundles of a hundred. That means five hundred pounds in each."

Wise nodded as he watched the money being stowed away.

"It's quite heavy," the clerk averred solemnly, as he passed the holdall back. "Got it? Good morning, Mr. Fox."

As Wise returned to the van, he marvelled at the ease with which the operation had been accomplished. The clerk's complete lack of curiosity had been most gratifying. Presumably they were so used to dealing in huge sums that there was nothing remarkable in someone cashing a cheque for six thousand pounds, provided, of course, his account could stand it.

It was in a thoroughly sunny mood that he drove on to Earls Court. This time he parked the van even farther away from his destination than he had in Shepherd's Bush, and once more approached the bank on foot and minus the disguise he had adopted on the previous occasion.

The Southern Bank's premises were smaller than those of the United, with only one teller on duty during the lunch period. His name-plate proclaimed him to be Mr. J. Hilliard, and Wise studied him as he dealt with the preceding customer. He was around thirty, with a small, petulant rosebud mouth and a high forehead which gave him an air of haughtiness. His well-greased blond hair was brushed straight back without a parting and stood out spikily at the back.

The man ahead moved away from the counter and Wise lifted up the holdall. Mr. Hilliard looked at it with disdain.

"I want to pay this"—he nodded in the direction of the holdall—"into my account."

"Your name, please?"

"Carter, William Carter. I have an account at this branch."

"How much are you paying in, Mr. Carter?"

"Six thousand pounds. I'll make out a paying-in slip, shall I?" He spoke nonchalantly, and avoided looking at Mr. Hilliard as he reached for a pen. He was aware, however, of the clerk's gaze on him for a full minute before lifting the holdall his side of the counter and opening it.

"There are a hundred five-pound notes in each bundle," Wise said in a helpful tone as Mr. Hilliard damped his right forefinger and began to count. "Do you want me to stay while you do that?"

"It's in your interest, Mr. Carter, to see whether my arithmetic tallies with yours." He looked up with a small, superior smile and went on counting. Wise returned the smile and leaned casually on the counter.

In fact the whole proceeding took less time than he had expected, and with its completion Mr. Hilliard stamped the paying-in slip with resounding force and said, "It seems to have come out right first time, Mr. Carter."

Wise reached for the empty holdall and with a formal goodbye departed. He hadn't cared for Mr. J. Hilliard, and it had been a strain standing there watching him coldly counting the money. At least he hadn't made any inquisitive observations, though Wise

23

now realised that such would have amounted to unwarranted impertinence and been altogether unlikely. Bank clerks learn discretion before book-keeping.

In the few weeks that William Carter's account had been open Wise had been careful to feed it with cash. No cheque had ever passed through it, so that none of its credits—all small ones until today—could ever be traced. It had been his practice to draw cash cheques on his Peter Fox account every so often and send the banknotes by registered post to his William Carter account. And since William Carter's registered address with the bank was, in fact, an accommodation one, an unlicensed accommodation address at that, there was no risk of his being traced through it. Moreover, the old girl who ran it was near dotty, which further excluded the possibility of detection. On occasions he would reverse the procedure by drawing cash from Carter's account and paying it into Fox's. He had felt that it was important to operate his two false accounts with fair regularity, so that, when the time came, the rapid movement—almost a flit, one might say—of six thousand pounds would be less likely to attract attention at either bank.

But now the money was securely lodged where it couldn't be traced, and stage one of his master-plan for self-enrichment was accomplished.

A confectioner's caught his eye and he went in and bought some not very good chocolates in a richly ornate box. By the time Lesley Gracey had eaten those Stage Two would have been executed. He smiled at the aptness of the word.

4

When the alarm clock woke him on Friday morning Wise couldn't, in the first dawn of consciousness, think why he should be feeling different from any other morning; why he should be experiencing the same intoxicating sensation he had known as a child when a special treat was in store and the day had at last arrived. Then he remembered, and as if to savour the full stimulation of his thoughts he stayed in bed a couple of additional minutes.

He kicked off the bedclothes and moved rapidly into the bathroom, where he shaved—soap and water and a fresh blade—to cheerful music supplied by the transistor set he kept there. The process of getting up occupied exactly twelve minutes, including the making of his bed, which he always did with care and thoroughness. Not for him the hasty rearrangement of crumpled sheets and twisted blankets. Next into the kitchen to cook his breakfast and an extra fried egg for his midday sandwich. He always gave himself a good breakfast, and this morning it was an extra good one since he reckoned that he would be burning up his resources of nervous energy at an increased rate: and, moreover, was unlikely to snatch much sleep during the coming night.

Shortly after eight o'clock he left the flat and walked up the road to catch his bus. It was a fifteen-minute ride to work and he had never once been late. More often than not he arrived before Mr. Gracey himself and had to hang about the yard until his employer appeared a minute or two before the half-hour. It was so on this Friday morning.

"You've got a full day, haven't you?" Mr. Gracey asked, as he unlocked the back door of the shop.

"Yes."

"I believe Mrs. Gracey's made you two further appointments. Be able to fit them in?"

"I expect so. Where are they?"

Mr. Gracey turned a page of the desk diary and, lifting his spectacles up on to his forehead, squinted at the scrawled list of appointments for the day. His wife's entries were inclined to be descriptively simple, frequently vague and usually inaccurate.

Addressing the room at large, Mr. Gracey read out, "Jenkinson, loose wire inside. Hubbard, queer sound. Campbell, picture giggles . . . no jiggles." "Jiggling pictures" was one of Mrs. Gracey's more favoured diagnostic descriptions. "Duncan, set too hot." Mr. Gracey snorted. "Sounds like a bloody bowl of soup. And what the devil's this? Mrs. Sankey can't switch off." He sighed. "Doesn't sound as though many of those'll be jobs you can do on the spot—and I'm just about full up in the workshop too."

This morning, ritual over—Mrs. Gracey herself never arrived until half-past nine, when the shop opened—Wise got the van out and set off first to see what could be done about Mr. Jenkinson's loose wire inside.

It had begun to rain heavily and he hoped earnestly it was going to be nothing more than a shower. If it rained all day . . . He scanned the skies with all the anxiety of a cricket enthusiast. The weather was one thing against which his plans couldn't be guarded. However, with the completion of his last call in the late afternoon, it had been raining off and on the whole time, and everywhere looked well washed. He had just parked the van in the yard when Lesley Gracey materialised at the driver's door.

"Hello, Colin."

"Hello, Lesley. Here." He reached for the box of chocolates. "I've bought you a present."

"Ooh, thank you, Colin," she crooned. "What a beautiful box!"

"I hoped you'd like it. You do eat chocolates, don't you?"

"I'm not meant to, they make me spotty, but that doesn't matter. It's the thought. It's the first present you've ever given me," she said with a smile of delight.

26

"No, it isn't," he replied staunchly. "I gave you a brooch for Christmas."

"Not counting that. It's the first non-Christmas, non-birthday present you've given me."

"It's a sort of earnest of my good intentions."

"What's that mean?"

"That I haven't forgotten I'm going to invite you to my flat."

Her face lit up and she hugged the box to her. "You must get awfully lonely living by yourself?"

"No."

"What do you do when you get home in the evenings?"

"Lots of things."

"Such as?"

"Cooking, eating, tidying up and going to bed," he said with a grin.

"But those are all women's jobs."

"Men eat, too!"

"You know what I mean," she protested. "Wouldn't you like to be married?"

"I'm waiting for the right girl," he said lightly, and then, observing her suddenly dreamy expression, wished he hadn't. "Out of the way, Lesley," he went on in a brisk tone. "I've still got work to do."

She moved aside and he opened the door.

"What are you doing this evening?" she asked, as though a sudden thought had occurred to her.

"The things I mentioned just now," he said guardedly.

"But it's Friday."

"That doesn't make it any different." *Except that I'm going to kill a man tonight*, he thought.

"I don't have any homework on Fridays." He pretended not to have heard, but braced himself for what he knew was coming next. "I could come in and do your cooking and tidying up." She went on excitedly, "I'm quite a good cook. Mummy often leaves me to prepare the supper at home." She looked up at him eagerly. "Would you like me to, Colin?"

He swallowed. "Not this evening, Lesley. I'm not sociable on Friday evenings. End-of-week exhaustion. . . ." He managed

27

to give her a wan smile. "And, anyway, when you do come I'm going to show *you* what sort of a cook *I* am."

"But I'd love to help you. I don't want to be treated like a guest. I'd sooner——"

"On your first visit you'll be a guest," he said firmly.

Mr. Gracey's voice now broke in on what was rapidly becoming an unmanageable conversation. "Stop gabbing and come and give me a hand, Colin."

"See, now I'm in trouble with your father," he said with a grimace. "Be good, Lesley. See you next week." He carefully emphasised the word "next" and hurried across to the workshop to find his employer looking unusually grumpy.

"How long've you been out there?"

"Only a few minutes."

"Lesley spends too much time hanging around here. I'd sooner you didn't encourage her."

The unfairness of the rebuke so stung Wise that he was temporarily blind to its irony and said with considerable feeling, "I don't give her any encouragement. As a matter of fact I find her attentions a trifle embarrassing."

No sooner were the words out than he could have choked himself, for not only did Mr. Gracey's features take on a meaner cast but he was aghast at having allowed himself to be provoked into indiscretion. His nerves must be under a greater strain than he was aware of. He held out a hand and studied it. Not a tremor; nevertheless he must take a grip on himself and watch out. This was no moment to start betraying himself. For better or for worse—and Wise wasn't certain which—Mr. Gracey made no further comment on the matter, and for the next half hour they worked in a heavy silence.

To make up for his lapse, Wise, who was never a shirker, threw himself with extra zest into the job in hand and was glad to see that his employer noticed this. He even worked past his normal hour without any sidelong glances at the clock. By the time they had finished it was nearly half-past six and he felt that atonement was complete.

"You can leave the van, I'll put it away later," Mr. Gracey remarked as Wise was preparing to leave.

"But you said I could borrow it this evening," Wise said, in a voice as calm as he could make it.

"I don't remember that."

"I mentioned it on Monday and you said it would be all right."

"Well, it's not. Anyway, what do you want it for?"

To transport a body, he'd have liked to have ground out in Mr. Gracey's stupid face. Instead: "To go and fetch a chair I've bought in a sale."

"Ah!" Mr. Gracey's grunt indicated a first glimmering of recollection. Wise waited, his teeth and muscles clenched in a mixture of anger and dismay, while his employer moved aimlessly about the workshop ignoring him.

How in heaven's name was he going to manage without the van at this short notice? He supposed he could always use Goodwin's own car, but this in itself would involve a further adjustment of his plans. He threw a venomous look at Mr. Gracey's back as he bent over to tie a shoe-lace. He would happily have throttled him at this moment if retribution hadn't appeared so certain.

"You can help me load this set into the van," Mr. Gracey said, moving off into a far corner. Wise followed him. He had no alternative.

"Where's it to go?" he asked flatly.

"To my place." Mr. Gracey said nothing further until the set was in the van and he had locked up for the night. "You'll have to come with me first and you can have the van afterwards."

"Thanks," Wise said, hardly trusting himself to keep the savage edge out of his tone.

What a start to the most crucial evening of his life!

*   *   *   *   *

The telephone was ringing when Wise opened the front door and managed somehow to give the impression that it had been doing so for a long time. He received even fewer calls than he made, and was now filled with foreboding as he ran up the stairs.

His "hello" was hoarse and tentative as he lifted the receiver.

"That you, Colin? Geoffrey Goodwin here."

29

Wise had recognised the voice immediately, and his sense of foreboding deepened.

"Good evening, Mr. Goodwin," he said, with far greater cheerfulness than he felt.

A sneeze exploded down the line. "I'm starting a cold, Colin, and I doubt whether I'm a very welcome guest anywhere this evening." Wise realised that a response was called for, but he could only stand paralysed and gripping the telephone receiver with unconscious ferocity. "Hello . . . are you still there, Colin?"

"Yes. Yes, Mr. Goodwin, I'm here." Suddenly the words began to pour out of him. "Please do come, even if only for half an hour. I'm not afraid of catching your cold, and it's quite a warm evening. . . . I shall be terribly disappointed if you don't. . . . I've got everything ready. . . . I've even bought a bottle of that liqueur you like. It is Green Chartreuse, isn't it? I've also got . . . well, got a small farewell present I was hoping you would like." He searched his mind feverishly. "It's a picture or rather a drawing—one of mine which I've had specially framed." *That was a good touch for the spur of the moment.* "Please come if only for a short while."

"I'm afraid it will only be for a short while." Goodwin's tone indicated a faint resentment at having been out-manœuvred. He had clearly expected Wise to release him readily from his social obligation. Instead, he had been subjected to a relentless moral pressure which no man with a conscience could have withstood.

Wise leaned against the wall with relief. "I promise I won't try and keep you when you want to leave." *That was a laugh.* "I'll still expect you around half-past eight."

"O.K. But don't blame me if you go down with a streaming cold." In a resigned tone he went on, "I've been on the run all day, so perhaps another outing won't do me all that much harm. But you shouldn't have gone to such a lot of trouble. Well, see you in just over an hour."

Replacing the receiver, Wise flopped down into a chair. He felt as though he had just run five miles in boots made of lead; he was clammy all over and aware of the thumping of his heart. If Goodwin *had* refused to come, there'd have been nothing for

it but for him to have gone to Goodwin. . . . Stealthily, un-
invited. . . . As he rose to go and change, he congratulated himself on the speed with which he had mustered his wits and
righted a tricky situation. It was a good augury; it showed he
was capable of surmounting a sudden crisis.

By the time he had washed and changed his equanimity was
restored and he found himself taking particular relish in the last-
minute preparations. As he busied himself about the room he
could almost have been a young man out to impress his future
mother-in-law on her first visit. He plumped up the cushions,
gave the curtains an adjusting shake, straightened the shade of
the standard lamp, and finally put out the coffee cups and two
liqueur glasses. When all was ready in the living-room he went
into the kitchen and lit a flame under the coffee-pot—and waited.

It was twenty minutes to nine when he heard a car door being
slammed and ran through to the living-room to look out of the
window. He saw Goodwin enter the yard with the diffident
movements of someone unsure whether he's come to the right
address. Hurrying down the stairs, he flung open the front door
to confront a surprised guest.

"I heard your car," he explained. "You didn't have any
difficulty finding your way?"

"None, thanks to your explicit instructions." Goodwin
entered and began to mount the stairs. "You're nicely tucked
away down here, aren't you?"

"Yes, it's very quiet."

"I see you use your employer's van for travelling to and
fro."

"Not really; just depends." Almost shyly he ushered Goodwin
into the living-room and anxiously watched for his reaction.
For some bizarre reason he did genuinely want him to be impressed.

"You've made this room charming, Colin," Goodwin said,
looking about him appreciatively. "If you ever give up repair-
ing television sets you could become an interior decorating
consultant." He walked across to where one of Wise's drawings
hung on the wall. It was of Marble Arch and one of the first
he had done on coming to London. "I like that." He turned

31

to Wise with a deprecating smile. "Am I allowed to see the one you said you're going to give me?"

Wise froze. He had clean forgotten that particular blandishment. And now there was only one choice.

"I'll go and fetch it," he said awkwardly, and left the room. He went into his bedroom and took the drawing of Lincoln's Inn Fields off the wall. What did it matter? It'd be back there again in an hour or so. Holding it in front of him, he returned to Goodwin.

"Oh, I like that very much, Colin," Goodwin said enthusiastically. "And I know exactly where I'll hang it. On the landing at the top of the stairs." He took the picture from Wise and examined it at arm's length. "How many more like this have you done?"

"A dozen or so, but most of them are not finished."

"Nevertheless, I'd like to see them."

"I'll get the coffee," he said abruptly. When he returned to the room, Goodwin was still standing in the middle studying his picture.

"Doesn't this fine work ruin your eyes?"

"Not yet. Black or white, Mr. Goodwin?"

"Oh, black please."

Goodwin moved towards the sofa which was against the wall.

"No, you sit in that chair," Wise said quickly, "it's more comfortable."

"The sofa looks all right," Goodwin said in surprise, but sat down where he was told. "How did you know that Green Chartreuse was my favourite liqueur?"

"I saw a bottle in your house."

"But there are other ones there, too."

"Er . . . I think you probably mentioned it." He smiled disarmingly. "Anyway, I did know."

In fact he had noticed that, whereas most of the other bottles of liqueur were virtually full, there was not much Green Chartreuse left. From this he had deduced, rightly as it turned out, that the prettiest was also the favourite.

When the coffee and liqueurs had been dispensed, a certain restraint seemed to settle over the room. Goodwin, who became aware of it, assumed it was due to the new relationship (host and guest) which had temporarily replaced their more normal one of disgruntled customer and television repair man. He supposed Wise might be feeling a trifle inhibited in his changed rôle, and that perhaps in this instance it was the duty of the guest to put the host at ease. Colin Wise, who was similarly aware of the atmosphere of restraint, knew that it was due to the imminence of what was to come. The waiting was notoriously the worst part of any enterprise and he didn't intend that it should be prolonged. But there were still one or two things he must find out before killing Goodwin. He drained his coffee cup in a single gulp and poured himself out another.

"What time are you off tomorrow?" he asked in a distant voice.

"My plane leaves at half-past three. I shall get to the airport about an hour before that."

"Do you drive yourself there?"

"No, I shall take a taxi."

Wise noted the reply with satisfaction. He had thought it possible that Goodwin might already have made some arrangement which would require to be cancelled, but he apparently hadn't and that was to the good.

"Do you leave your car in your garage all the time you're away?"

"No, the local people are coming to fetch it on Monday and give it a thorough service. When they put it back, they'll disconnect the battery and do the various other things for laying it up."

"What about Hilda? Does she come in and look after the cottage while you're away?"

"Yes, she'll keep an eye on the place. Incidentally, she's taken a fancy to you. I rather think she was glad my set broke down so often." Wise pulled a wry face, and Goodwin went on, "So you'd better watch out if you come to the house again when I get back. I shall be vexed if you're the cause of my losing an admirable housekeeper."

"She could be my grandmother."

"I dare say, but she's a widow, so watch out."

Wise grinned. "I expect she'll be fussing around you to-morrow, making sure you don't forget anything."

"We went through all that today." Goodwin shifted his chair. "Now show me the rest of the flat, Colin."

"Sure. Do you mean she's not coming in tomorrow?"

"Uh?" Goodwin had risen and was looking about the room.

"Hilda—not coming in?"

"No," he said, his mind clearly elsewhere; then, "I like the shade of this carpet."

"I thought she usually did on Saturdays."

"What? . . . Oh, Hilda. You seem to have got her on the brain! She does usually come in on Saturdays but not tomorrow. She's had a couple of grandchildren dumped on her for the week-end. And if you want to know their names, they're Jacqueline and Kenneth."

Though he had now gleaned all the information he required, Wise blushed, "I'm awfully sorry. I wasn't meaning to be in-quisitive about Hilda. . . ." He had a sudden flash of inspiration. "It was just that I was wondering whether there was anything *I* could do to help tomorrow. Help carry luggage or drive you to the airport. . . ."

It was Goodwin's turn to look embarrassed. "That's awfully good of you, Colin, but I don't think there's anything. It's all under control. But, all the same, thanks for the offer. Now show me the rest of the flat and then your drawings, and after that"— he glanced at his watch—"I shall have to be going."

First they went into the bedroom, which Goodwin duly admired. "Used you to have a picture on that wall?" he asked, nodding in the direction of the naked nail which awaited the return of his "farewell present".

Without a flicker Wise replied, "Yes. The glass broke the other day and I'm waiting to buy a fresh piece."

Next the bathroom and then the kitchen received Goodwin's appreciative comments. As they returned to the living-room, he said, "You really have made it delightful, Colin. I congratulate you."

"Sit down and have a drop more liqueur and I'll fetch my

drawings," Wise said. Then as Goodwin moved toward the sofa: "No, sit in this chair. You'll find the light better."

Leaving his guest ensconced, he left the room. The moment had almost arrived and he instinctively patted his trouser pocket as he reached up for the folder of drawings on the top shelf of his wardrobe.

"Here they are!" He plumped the folder into Goodwin's lap and moved round behind the chair, ostensibly to lean over his guest and conduct him through the artistic world of Colin Wise. *I'll just give him time to get interested and then I'll . . .*

Goodwin suddenly leapt from the chair, and Wise recoiled in startled horror. He hadn't even made a move yet: Goodwin couldn't have seen into his mind.

"Damn, I've dropped my cigarette. There it is." Goodwin reached down. "Are you all right, Colin?" he asked anxiously, catching sight of his host's expression.

"Yes, I'm all right," Wise said dully. *Just shaken to the roots, that's all.*

"You look terribly pale. You'd better sit down. Come on, we'll go and sit on the sofa."

"No. I'll be all right. It's . . . it's just a touch of stomach cramp. I'm better if I stand up." *God boy, you're having to do some fast thinking this evening.*

Goodwin sat down again—and, encouraged by Wise, turned to the first drawing.

"That's just a working sketch I made but never got any further with."

"Somerset House, is it?"

"Yes."

"Always seems to me it's such an attractive building to house such disagreeable activities. Or part of it does, anyway." He looked round and, misinterpreting Wise's blank expression, added, "Inland Revenue Department."

Wise nodded abstractedly and reached for the length of tough cord in his trouser pocket. "The next one I intend to do something about. It's one of those terraces up Regent's Park way," he said, turning the page for his guest and standing back.

Goodwin obligingly bent forward to study the drawing. "Yes, I like that. I think . . ."

He got no farther, for at that moment the cord was whipped over his head and drawn right round his neck. His last sound was of steam escaping under pressure as his hands flew up too late to save himself. A foot kicked out desperately and sent his liqueur glass and coffee-cup spinning off the table in front of him. Wise, who had been pulling on the two ends of the cord with his teeth clenched and his eyes tightly shut, looked down to see what had happened and cursed softly as he saw two ugly stains on the pale carpet. He peered into Goodwin's face and then away in distaste. Strangulation does not improve the complexion, and it didn't require any doctor to certify that Goodwin was dead.

Leaving him slumped in the chair, Wise went into the kitchen to fetch a floor-cloth and spent the next few minutes rubbing vigorously at the marks on the carpet. It was his latest acquisition—a pale mushroom shade—and he was filled with resentment at Goodwin's heedless convulsion which had caused the damage. Why did he have to kick in that direction? Why did he have to kick at all? Why couldn't he have died without those last futile flutterings? Satisfied that he had done all that was possible for the time being—he'd only be able to decide if additional treatment was necessary when it had dried—he put the things away and turned his attention to Goodwin's inert form.

First he removed his shoes and socks (easy); then his trousers and underpants (more difficult); finally his jacket, tie and shirt (a struggle). Leaving the undressed body crumpled on the floor, he folded the clothes tidily, emptying the pockets and making a neat pile of the contents. These he then sorted with care, putting keys and money on one side, and pocket diary and wallet, both of which he proposed to destroy, separately. He failed to find Goodwin's air tickets or anything relating to his journey to Australia, and assumed he must have left these at home. The wallet contained nothing of interest, just the usual assortment of membership cards, a driving licence, a car insurance certificate and a book of stamps. He'd burn all of them. A quick look through the pocket diary showed that it contained nothing of significance, merely notes of appointments such as lunch and

36

dinner dates and the like, and a list of telephone numbers at the end.

He was now ready for the next move, and after eyeing Goodwin's corpse thoughtfully for a second or two, trying to make up his mind which would be the easier method of portage, he bent down, and, looping his arms beneath the dead man's, he began to back out of the room. He was pleased to note that Goodwin's feet dragging on the carpeted floor made no marks that a brush wouldn't remove, and that he had obviously tackled the job from the right end. He was about half-way along the passage when the telephone rang.

If the archangel had come suddenly through a skylight Wise could not have been more transfixed by surprise. Halting abruptly in his tracks, he stood listening and wondering what to do. His mind surveyed all the possible callers while the bell continued its monotonous summons. If he answered it, heavens knew what unknown digressions he might be drawn into, what incalculable consequences might flow from the very act of lifting the receiver. And if he didn't? Well, the odds were that it was a wrong number, anyway; but if not, the somebody would assume he was not at home—and, after all, there was no reason why he should be.

He took a fresh grip on Goodwin and set off again on his backward journey to the bathroom. Goodwin! Was it possible that he had told a friend where he was going to be for the evening and that the phone was ringing for him? Wise broke out in a cold sweat and lowered the body to the floor. He went back into the living-room and stared impotently at the telephone. Why didn't the bloody thing stop ringing! If only he could silence it as he had silenced Goodwin. It was getting him down with its never-ending brr-brr, brr-brr, brr-brr. It was possessed of a devil. Who on earth could show such crazy determination to get an answer?

And then suddenly it stopped; and in the palpable silence which followed, Colin Wise wiped his face and hands on his handkerchief and poured himself out a brandy, then another. He felt better after that.

Not like you, Colin, to let your nerves get all jazzed up. You're right, but it was the spookiness of it coming at that particular moment. Well, have another brandy and see it doesn't happen again.

He returned fortified to where Goodwin's body lay in the passage, and a couple of minutes later had manhandled it through the door and into the bath. Then he went into his bedroom and, stripping down to his underpants, put on an old sleeveless sports shirt, which he was prepared to sacrifice if necessary. Thus incongruously dressed, he fetched a long sharp knife from the kitchen and returned to the bathroom.

Wise had given considerable thought to the disposal of his victim's body, and, having finally decided on dismemberment and a wide dispersal of the portions, he had given as much thought again to this aspect of his task.

In the event, the cutting up of the body took him rather less time than he had expected—only just over an hour, with a couple of breaks for further recourse to the brandy—and proved not to be as messy a job as he had thought it might be. Nevertheless, it wasn't one he performed with any relish. He regarded it simply as a disagreeable task which was necessary to his plans and in which the end more than justified the means. In this spirit he had gone to work. . . .

When he had finished, he went downstairs and fetched several large sheets of heavy, waterproof paper such as is seen on construction sites, some sacking and a number of large polythene bags. It took him an hour and a half to parcel up the portions of Goodwin's body. The head presented no difficulty, but legs and torsos are not prone to tidy wrapping and he was quite exhausted by the time he had finished. Then one by one he carried the parcels downstairs and stowed them carefully into the back of Mr. Gracey's van. The head he first placed in an old oil drum containing a small quantity of acid which he had scrounged from Mr. Gracey's workshop. One note of minor relief had been to observe that Goodwin had no particular distinguishing marks on his body, apart from a couple of ordinary moles on his back. And who doesn't have moles on his back? thought Wise. Nevertheless, he had no intention that any of the pieces of body should ever be found.

He returned upstairs and set about cleaning the bath. Both

taps were already running, and he now gave it a thorough scrubbing all over. He clucked annoyance as he noticed the small scratches his butchery had caused on the bottom of the bath, and there was also a long score mark on the side where the knife had suddenly slipped.

When no removable trace remained he filled the bath almost to the brim and emptied two pints of cheap Eau de Cologne into the water. Then, pulling out the plug, he watched it drain away, till the final gurgle wound its way down the waste-pipe. The bathroom smelt fresh and sweet and no one could have guessed at the gruesome deed which had just been performed there.

He had washed the knife and now took this back to the kitchen, fingering its still sharp blade with new respect. He felt no squeamishness at the prospect of its reversion to normal use.

It was just on midnight when, dressed once more, he was ready for the next stage. Midnight! God, he wasn't going to have much time to spare! He'd be lucky if he got to bed at all.

He dashed into the living-room and parcelled up Goodwin's clothes and effects, apart from his keys and money, which he thrust into his own trouser pocket. Locking the clothes into the back of the van and securing the gate of the yard, he got into Goodwin's car and was about to set course for the cottage near Fulmer, when, with his finger actually on the starter button, he paused and put his hands up to his head. He must think and quickly. He wasn't merely pressed for time, it was now going to be virtually impossible to achieve all he had set himself to do. And not virtually impossible. Impossible. How could he have miscalculated so badly. It was difficult to think clearly with the forerunners of sudden panic nibbling at his mind.

Concentrate, Wise; think, man. If you can't manage both facets of your nocturnal operations, what to do? Think it out, fellow; think it out. But quickly, minutes are slipping by.

Stiffly, painfully, and with a feeling of growing anxiety, he realised that the important thing was to rid himself of the body. That meant he'd have to retain Goodwin's car and return it tomorrow night. He remembered that Hilda wasn't going to the cottage again before the weekend and that the garage people weren't due to collect the car till Monday, so perhaps everything would be all right after all. He'd still have to call there some-time tonight, however, for he had to remove Goodwin's luggage and tickets before daybreak.

Trying hard to calm his fears, he backed the van out of the yard and parked Goodwin's car in its place. He hoped that any-one who heard the noise would assume it was the break-up of a party. At least there wasn't anyone in view.

He felt a measure of relief as he drove along the almost deserted main road. Driving invariably relaxed him—even, apparently, with a body in the back. In his mind he went through and ticked off the various points in the impending body-disposal operation. By the time he reached his first port of call, a large wood, his confidence was restored, and he was feeling quite cheerful again.

He parked the van beneath some tall trees, turned off the lights and, rather like a delivery man, fetched one of the parcels from the back of the van. It was one containing a leg. With this under one arm and a spade in his free hand, he clambered through a gap in the hedge and walked about twenty-five yards into the wood.

Rain had softened the ground, and digging was easier than it would have been the previous night. It still took him forty minutes, however, to bury the parcel and cover the traces. He had carefully selected an area where the soil was largely peat, and this meant not only lighter digging but a more irregular surface appearance to disguise his activities.

About a mile and a half farther away in another part of the same wood he buried the second leg. He regained the van and set off on an eight-mile cross-country journey, which took him into the Chilterns, and for the last half-mile along a track which ran between high hedges until it suddenly petered out on the grassy top of a small hill. He drove this final stretch on sidelights only, and even switched these off just before he reached the summit.

Clutching to him the large and uncomfortably heavy parcel containing Goodwin's torso and arms, he staggered forward fifteen yards to where a shaft disappeared into the ground. Balancing it on the rim for a second, he then rolled it over the edge and stood listening for the distant muffled thud which would tell him it had reached its resting-place.

He had come across the shaft by accident on a weekend walk and remembered it when he came to consider how to dispose of Goodwin's body. He had then made a proper reconnaissance and found it ideal for his purpose.

It was a ventilator shaft for a now disused railway tunnel which ran beneath the hill. Experiments with pebbles had told him that it had a kink in it about forty feet down, and he had subsequently confirmed this by walking through the tunnel and ascertaining that daylight wasn't visible when you peered up from below.

He went back to the van with a still lighter heart and paused to inhale deeply the clean night air before he got back in. It was half-past two. Not far away an owl made his mournful call, followed by the hectic squeaks of his prey. Having been brought up in the country, Wise enjoyed listening to all the nocturnal sounds of nature which always surrounded the human intruder. With a tug of reluctance he opened the van door and got in.

With the lights off, he made a sweeping turn on to the open grass, and was about to head into the dark yawning gully where the track began, when the van made a sudden lurch to the left and the rear wheels spun wildly. Colin Wise groaned aloud.

Putting the vehicle into reverse he gingerly let in the clutch. For a second it seemed it was going to respond, but then the wheels flew crazily round again. He thrust the van savagely into first gear—he'd make it take off like a rocket—let the clutch in with a bang, at the same time accelerating hard. But these shock tactics only served to convince him that he was well and truly stuck. He clambered out to examine his predicament. In his mind's eye he saw himself still marooned there as dawn broke, only a few yards from evidence which would put him on a conveyer belt to the gallows and with the countryside coming to life all about him.

A sense of desperation added urgency to his quest for anything which would assist his escape. The hedge seemed to offer the best possibility, and he cut several armfuls from it and packed these beneath the rear wheels. Hardly daring to breathe, he started the engine up and eased the van forwards in second gear. The wheels seemed to be gripping and he increased pressure on the accelerator. With a feeling of immeasurable relief he steered it on to the hard shoulder of the hill and halted. He must do his best to conceal the evidence of his presence.

The pieces of hedge went down the shaft, and the spade helped to obliterate the deep troughs excavated by the rear wheels.

He didn't begin to breathe normally again until fifteen minutes later, when he was back on the main Oxford-London road and heading for what was perhaps the most degrading of all the burial spots he had chosen for Goodwin's dismembered body. This was a field of junk, of derelict metal which had once been motor-cars, and—in one corner which had attracted Wise's attention to it—of an ever-growing mound of old oil drums. Indeed, it was in one of these oil drums that Goodwin's head now rested in the back of the van.

He parked at the entrance to the field, lifted the drum out and carried it with abnormal care to where several hundred of them rose in an irregular pyramid. A small amount of rearrangement ensured it a place at the rear, beneath the others, so that anyone on the scrounge would be extremely unlikely to come upon it.

This done, he ran back to the van, stimulated by the completion—the successful completion despite the setbacks—of this phase of his plan. Tired, sticky and filthily dirty though he was, he had still to visit Goodwin's cottage. However, it shouldn't take him more than a quarter of an hour to drive there at this time of night, and with luck ten minutes should be sufficient to accomplish what he had to do.

It was a quarter to four, and in just under a couple of hours it would be beginning to get light. Would this night never end? had been his one-time thought. All too soon, it now seemed.

He removed his shoes and left them in the porch. They were caked with mud, and he had no wish to leave a trail all over the cottage for faithful Hilda to find on Monday morning. He opened the door with Goodwin's key, and then paused in the hall to get his bearings. It was warm and his nose twitched as

42

it savoured the now familiar smells of the place. It gave him a curiously awed feeling to think that its owner would never return. And Goodwin would have had more than a curious feeling if he could have foreseen events when he left home.

As his eyes grew accustomed to the darkness, he began to move stealthily upstairs. Though he had never been there before, he knew which was Goodwin's bedroom. Drawing the curtains, he turned on a light. Even if someone should notice it, there was nothing untoward in the showing of a bedroom light at four o'clock in the morning.

He was gratified to observe that Goodwin's packing was virtually completed. Three large suitcases full of clothes lay open on the floor, awaiting only the last-minute receipt of random items. On the dressing-table was a travel bag, and beside it a large, bulging black wallet. Wise examined this to find it contained Goodwin's tickets, cheque book, passport, vaccination certificate and a letter from B.O.A.C. giving details of flight schedules. He put it in his pocket and went into the bathroom. Gathering up all the likely-looking washing and shaving tackle, he returned to the bedroom and thrust them into one of the suitcases. Then hair-brushes and a pigskin case containing nail-scissors and the like which were obviously put out to be packed.

The bed was turned down and a pair of candy-striped pyjamas lay on top of the eiderdown. Wise flung these also into one of the cases and stood for a moment pondering what to do about the bed. Whatever state Hilda would expect to find it in on Monday morning certainly would not be as it now appeared. He'd have to make an intelligent guess and take a chance. The only way to make a bed appear slept in was to get right into it. Flinging off his outer garments he climbed between the sheets and rolled about. While he was dressing again he gave the pillow a few biffs and then paused to ponder again. Would Goodwin be more likely to leave the bedclothes pulled down to the bottom, or, since Hilda wouldn't be coming until forty-eight hours after his departure, would he possibly pull them back up? Being the fastidious person he was, Colin Wise knew which he would do. Finally, however, he decided to leave them in an untidy mound at the foot of the bed.

43

He carried two of the suitcases downstairs and returned for the remaining one and the travel bag. Then he switched out the light, remembering to draw back the curtains, and left the luggage in a pile in the hall while he went to take a quick look round the ground-floor. The kitchen revealed nothing untoward, nor yet the living-room. In the small study the blank face of the television set greeted him like a long-lost friend, but he had no further interest in it. Turning his attention to the desk, he went quickly through the drawers. There seemed to be nothing, however, which Goodwin might be expected to take with him. Furthermore, it seemed a fair assumption that all such items had already been put in his travel wallet.

All the downstairs curtains were drawn to and Wise decided to draw them back before leaving, otherwise the blacked-out appearance of the cottage might excite some passer-by's notice in the course of the day.

Five minutes later he was on his way home, and when just after five o'clock he glided to a halt outside the familiar gates he felt like a player in one of those indoor games which bristle with such imperatives as "Lose a turn", "Go back ten places" and "Pay all the other players a forfeit". One reached the finishing post exhausted. And that was only a game. The real thing was a thousand times worse.

He transferred Goodwin's cases to the boot of his car and locked them up. Another night's work still lay ahead.

5

When Mr. Gracey arrived to open up the premises that Saturday morning he found Wise in the yard busily engaged in washing the van. Wise had intended to have the job completed by the time his employer appeared, but it had taken longer than he had expected for the simple reason that the van was even dirtier when seen in the cold light of morning than he had feared it would be.

Mr. Gracey walked round the as yet untouched side of the van without saying a word, while Wise, who was sluicing water round the offside rear wheel, watched his movements with apprehension.

"Did you pick up the chair all right?" Mr. Gracey asked, coming round the front of the van. His tone was mild and Wise felt reassured.

"Yes thanks, Mr. Gracey. And thanks for the loan of the van."

But Mr. Gracey didn't appear to be listening. "Where was this chair?" he asked nastily. "In the middle of a ploughed field?"

Wise smiled ruefully. "I'm afraid it is in a bit of a mess. I . . . er . . . had to turn round up a lane. I missed my way and then had to back into a farm entrance . . ."

"In Ealing?" Mr. Gracey opened the driver's door and peered inside.

"Surprising though it is, there are still a few farms about in that area. Quite a bit of open land really. . . ." Wise left the sentence unfinished, as it was obvious that Mr. Gracey wasn't listening, couldn't even hear with his head inside the van.

When he withdrew it, he said sharply, "Were you driving about the whole night?"

45

"No! What makes you ask that?"

"You've been sixty-eight miles."

"That's nonsense, I can't have been," Wise replied emphatically. He'd have to bluff this out.

"Well, you have. I distinctly remember noticing the mileage thing read 17423 when you dropped me home last night. Now it's 17491."

"Either it's not working properly or you mis-read it. It's very easy to do," he added quickly. "But I certainly never drove sixty-eight miles." In fact he had been surprised that it hadn't been more. It had seemed more. Now let the old idiot check the tank if he wished, for he'd find it full.

Mr. Gracey glowered, but obviously didn't feel confident enough to refute Wise's flat contradiction. He opened the back of the van and looked suspiciously inside. Wise went on with his work and pretended not to notice. The first thing he had done had been to clean out the interior, not that there had been any tell-tale signs of his night's work to remove. Without a further word Mr. Gracey ambled off and unlocked the workshop.

When, a quarter of an hour later, Colin Wise had finished, he stuck his head round the door and said, "I'm off to Willesden, Mr. Gracey, to collect those spares for the twenty-one-inch sets. I should be back in about an hour."

Mr. Gracey grunted, and, with a triumphant look at his employer's reproachful rear, Wise departed. Shortly before he reached his destination, he pulled up at a telephone kiosk and put a call through to London Airport.

"This is Mr. Goodwin speaking," he announced when he was finally connected to the right extension. "I have a reservation on Flight BA 986, which I'm afraid I must now cancel."

"Just a moment please, sir. What was the name?"

"Goodwin. Geoffrey Goodwin."

"Yes, I have it, Mr. Goodwin. You now wish to reserve on a later flight?"

"Perhaps I could explain what's happened." Wise drew a deep breath. "I have to go over to Paris for a few days and I'd like to pick up a later flight somewhere en route, possibly Rome. I think BA 986 calls at Rome, doesn't it?"

"Yes it does. What day will you be wanting to travel on?"

"That's the trouble, I can't yet say. What I'd like to do is keep my ticket, and then when I arrive in Rome go to your office there and make a fresh reservation. That would be all right, wouldn't it?"

"Ye-es," the voice said doubtfully, "but how are you going to get to Paris? We can transfer you to BEA for your London-Paris-Rome flights and then you can rejoin one of our Australian flights at Rome. That would be best."

"Except that I have to go over to Paris by train."

"By train?" The voice could not have sounded more surprised if he had said by camel.

"Yes, I'm travelling with a friend who won't fly."

"Well, we'd better do it as you suggest, sir. We'll cancel your reservation for this afternoon and leave you to get in touch with our Rome office when you arrive."

"Thanks. Sorry to have given you all this trouble."

"That's quite all right, sir," the voice said equably, "we're used to this sort of thing."

Wise emerged from the call-box and expelled his breath in a noisy sigh of relief. Though lying was no problem and he could do so with fluency, he had no desire to be drawn further than absolutely necessary. The less you said, the less there was for anyone to remember, was an admirable maxim in present circumstances. He was pleased with his spiel about travelling overland to Paris, since this way Goodwin's supposed departure from the country would go officially unobserved. One feature of air travel (inhibiting for some) is the careful record of passengers' names kept on hideous purple lists, whereas a Channel port offers a comfortingly anonymous exit.

By the time he got back to Uxbridge Mr. Gracey seemed in better humour, though he remained less communicative than usual. Wise had a number of deliveries to make and so was able to keep out of his way for most of the morning.

One of his calls was at Miss Comber's—this time there was nothing wrong with her set, but he had received an enigmatic message asking that he should look in when he was next passing, and Mrs. Gracey had relayed the request without comment, for Miss Comber was a good customer.

"It's a little present I've bought you, Colin," she said in a fluttering voice as she invited him into the house. "I hope you'll like it." She picked up a parcel from the hall table and handed it to him. "Go on, open it now."

She watched him with eyes shining as eagerly as a child's at Christmas while he tore off the wrapping paper and took out a cashmere sweater. It was dark green with sleeves.

"You like it?"

"It's very nice, Miss Comber. Thank you."

"You've been so kind looking after my silly old set, I felt I wanted to give you something and I decided a sweater would probably be the most useful."

He was nonplussed by the present. He was never averse to getting what he could for nothing, but he had an unpleasant feeling that Miss Comber was putting him in her debt for an ulterior motive: that she had designs on his freedom; that, given half a chance, she'd have him at her beck and call. Well, no need to worry since she wasn't even going to be given an eighth of a chance.

"You will wear it?" she asked eagerly.

"Of course. It's a very nice one." He put it back in its box.

"And, Colin?"

"Yes, Miss Comber."

"That money I lent you, the twenty-five pounds, you needn't return it. I'd like you to regard that as a present too."

"Thank you," he said gravely. He could hardly add that he had never had any intention of repaying it. Miss Comber had been so insistent in her offers to lend him money that it had finally seemed stupid to refuse, so on five separate occasions he had said that he could do with five pounds when she had started up her twitter. He was really doing her a favour taking it, as she obviously got such a glow out of the whole business.

He said goodbye, and as he drove away saw her giving him little secret waves from the cover of her front door.

Thank goodness the morning was coming to an end. The lack of sleep was beginning to make itself felt, and as soon as the weekend shutters went up on Mr. Gracey's workshop at one o'clock he was heading for bed like a bear at the first sniff of winter. The shop remained open on Saturday afternoons, but he had to assist only on alternate ones. On the others Mr. Gracey gave his wife a hand.

His heart sank as he drove into the yard and saw Lesley talking to her mother in the little room at the back of the shop. What was worse, she immediately spotted him. Instead, however, of the happy smile she usually gave him he was aware of receiving the mournful look associated with dumb creatures parted from their young.

"Hello, Lesley," he said brightly as he climbed out. By this time she was standing beside the van so that the greeting was unavoidable.

"Hello," she replied gloomily, at the same time scanning his face as though trying to read a crystal ball.

He pretended to notice nothing strange in her behaviour. "I must go and see if your father wants me."

He turned but halted abruptly when the voice behind him laden with reproach said, "You weren't at home last night."

"Yes I was, I——"

"You weren't. I tried to phone you and there was no answer."

So it was you, you little wretch. He felt in no mood to propitiate her, but realised it would be expedient to do so.

"It must have been when I slipped out for a pint of beer."

"You said you'd be at home the whole evening. You said you were always tired on Friday evenings."

"I don't count having a pint of beer at the local as going out. I wasn't away more than a quarter of an hour."

"I tried to phone you later," she went on remorselessly, "and there was no answer that time either."

"Thought I heard the bell ring when I was in the bath," he answered with a grin.

She looked at him sulkily. "I thought you'd probably gone out with a girl."

"What were you phoning me for, anyway?" he asked, with a note of impatience.

49

"I just wanted to talk to you," she replied defensively. Then in a suddenly meek voice: "Will you be home this evening?"

"Probably not."

"Where are you going?"

"Look, Lesley, do I have to account to you for every move I make?"

The sulky, ill-used look returned to her face. "It was only yesterday you gave me a box of chocolates and said you were looking forward to my visiting you."

"I still am," he said, trying not to sound as edgy as he felt, "but no one likes being checked up on."

"I wasn't checking up on you. I was just asking in a conversational way what you were doing this evening."

"I haven't decided. Depends how I feel."

"Why don't we go out together?" she asked eagerly.

He shook his head. *Oh God, not through all this again!* Despair pervaded his spirit. "No, not tonight," he said wearily.

"Is something the matter, Colin?" Her tone was pointedly solicitous.

"Nothing." He conjured up a wan smile. "As a matter of fact I shall probably go to bed early tonight. I didn't sleep too well last night."

"You look rather pale," she agreed. "You wouldn't like me to call round and cook your supper?"

"No, I wouldn't, and for heaven's sake stop plaguing me so. I'll let you know when I need a cook," he burst out, and, turning on his heel, strode over to the workshop. When he looked out of the window she had disappeared. He bit his lip in annoyance. How did you shake off the attentions of a girl as persistent as that? He had tried both the extremes of kindness and coldness without apparent success. Why had she wanted to get a crush on him—for he was under no illusion that this was the nature of her ill? There were lots of other boys about. What perverse fate had made her cock her bonnet at the one man who was not merely indifferent but aggressively determined not to become ensnared by any personal relationship? There was no knowing how she might react now. The chocolates had proved a short-lived palliative. He almost wished he had dosed them with prussic acid. He turned away savagely from the window. He could only hope that he had succeeded in finally killing the unwanted and embarrassing relationship.

Mr. Gracey came into the workshop. "I thought you'd gone," he said. "I'm about to lock up. It's five past one."

Wise zipped up his jacket and walked out. He caught a bus home, and within five minutes of closing the front-door behind him was stretched asleep on top of his bed.

It was nearly seven o'clock when he awakened, and the street light at the end of the road came on as he stood stretching lazily in front of the window. He felt much better and decided to have a bath before getting himself a meal.

As he lay contentedly soaking, his eyes fell on one of the scratches he'd made the previous night. He frowned as, running a finger along it, he remembered there was another on the floor of the bath. He arched his back and felt beneath him. Yes, there it was, four inches long and the enamel deeply scored. How bloody annoying! The bath was almost new; and though the blemishes didn't affect its use, they did affront its user. And to make matters worse, there was probably nothing he could do about it short of buying another bath. Well, he wasn't going to do that, though he cheered himself with the thought that in his next home he'd have a bath which Elizabeth Taylor would be pleased to stretch in.

He had just finished dressing and was about to move into the kitchen when the phone rang. He could guess who it was.

"Yes?" he answered curtly.

"Colin, it's me, Lesley." Her tone was meek and submissive.

"What do you want?"

"I'm sorry I annoyed you this morning, I didn't mean to be nosy."

"That's all right, it's forgotten."

"You're not angry with me any more?"

"No."

"You don't sound as if you've forgiven me."

"For God's sake, Lesley, what do you want me to do, crawl along the line?"

"Have you decided what you're going to do this evening?"

"No."

"I haven't either," she said wistfully.

"That makes two of us," he said brutally.

"Did I tell you I showed the box of chocolates you gave me to my friend Rosemary?"

"I can't remember," he said in a bored tone.

"I told her a boy-friend had given them to me," she went on undaunted, "and Rosemary said you must be nice and I said you were."

"Is that so!"

"Will you do me a favour, Colin?"

"Not if you go on talking much longer."

"Will you give me a photograph of yourself?"

"I haven't any."

"Couldn't you get——"

"No, I couldn't," he broke in emphatically. "Now look, Lesley, I've got to go."

"I thought you said you hadn't decided what to do."

"There are still reasons for ending this chatter, so goodnight and have a nice weekend."

He put the receiver down without giving her an opportunity of fanning the conversation into life again. The sooner he left Mr. Gracey's employ and cleared right out of the district, the better. He was beginning to feel positively insecure with her around. There was no knowing where and when she mightn't pop up. However, if everything went well, he reckoned he should be able to up sticks in about a month, and after that Lesley Gracey would be no better remembered than a pimple on his face.

He went into the kitchen and scrambled some eggs and fried four rashers of bacon until they were crisp and brittle, the way he liked them. Two slices of buttered toast and a huge cup of coffee completed his meal.

It was just on half-past eight by the time he had finished washing up and putting everything away, and because it was still too early to embark on his next nocturnal operation he spent a further twenty minutes polishing the frying-pan until it gleamed like a newly minted coin.

Some time after this he fetched Goodwin's wallets, the one which he had removed from the dead man's jacket pocket and the larger travelling one containing his passport and tickets which he had taken from the cottage, and emptied their contents into the kitchen sink. Then he put a match to the small pile of documents and watched them buckle and wither in the flames. It required stern will-power to destroy an air ticket worth nearly a thousand pounds, but he knew it had to be. Greed was one thing, stupid greed quite another. When only ashes remained he turned on both taps and left them running until no trace of the miniature conflagration remained.

He now went downstairs and lifted the suitcases from the boot of Goodwin's car and laid them on the floor of the garage. He had deliberately refrained from examining their contents as there was no point in torturing himself. To keep so much as one sock could hang him. How often murderers convicted themselves by retaining items of property identified as their victims'! But not Colin Wise.

Armed with a heavy screw-driver, he proceeded to punch holes in the top and sides of the three suitcases and also in the travel bag. He reckoned that this should effectively deny them any tendency to float, for he had decided to dispose of them in the canal which ran through a factory area two miles from where he lived.

He had selected a stretch where a footbridge crossed the canal and where it was bounded on one side by a few desolate acres of wasteland and on the other by the rear of a small castings foundry. He had been there late at night on a couple of occasions and there had not been a soul about. Moreover, there was a handy place to park the car.

It was half-past one before he decided to set out on his mission. Then, leaving the car with the suitcases still in it, he approached the bridge with all the stealth of a commando patrol leader. Not until he had reconnoitred both sides of the canal in each direction was he satisfied that it was safe to go ahead. There was something eerily silent about the atmosphere which seemed filled with strange, rather frightening shapes. He wanted to get away from the place, and he shivered as he made his way back

53

to the car to fetch the cases. He'd always had a mild horror of water at night. It held mysterious power and was darkly secretive, and on the rare occasions he experienced a nightmare it was always of stepping over the edge of a quayside and falling thirty screaming feet into the sinister depths below.

Leaning as far over the bridge as possible, he released the largest of the cases. There was a splash and a lot of bubbles as the water closed over it, then only ripples lapping the bank and finally silence. The second case he cast over the opposite side of the bridge and it, too, vanished in seconds without trace. The third, which was the lightest, he threw into the middle of the canal from the towpath about twenty-five yards from the bridge. He was about to follow suit with the travel bag when it occurred to him that even with holes in it it'd be more likely to float than the heavier pieces. There were a number of large stones in the area and he inserted a couple. Then, hurling it from him, he watched its dark shape arc through the air and land in the middle of the canal, where it promptly sank.

He hurried back to the car to set off on the final lap of his pilgrimage of disposal. He had driven barely a hundred yards when a policeman on a bicycle came round a corner and passed him with a hard stare. Wise accelerated and made a quick turn to get out of sight. But it had been a near thing. If he'd been there another five minutes the policeman must surely have come upon him or, worse still, have heard the sound of splashes. Then there'd have to have been some rapid thinking—some rapid action too. For a few seconds he felt as though his insides had been scooped out. It was the shock of the unexpected. Well, thank goodness it was now almost all over.

When he arrived at Goodwin's cottage he drove straight up to the garage, unlocked it with the key which was on the same ring as the ignition key, and put the car away. It was only as he silenced the engine and switched off the lights that he realised he had no idea what arrangement Goodwin had made with the local garage over the keys. He could leave the ignition key in the car, but that wasn't going to help anyone gain entry into the locked garage. Supposing Goodwin had said he'd leave the garage key with them before he departed . . . Well, he hadn't, and if Wise were to remedy that now they'd know it had been put through their letter-box after they'd closed on Saturday night—that is, after Goodwin was supposed to be out of the country. That wouldn't really matter, however; they'd probably accept that he'd forgotten and given it to a friend to drop at their premises. So that's what he'd do. But then it came to him that he didn't know the name of the garage with whom Goodwin dealt. After further cogitation, he decided there was only one course open to him and that was to detach the garage key from the ring and leave it in the lock. Even if they did look somewhere else first, they must eventually find it. They'd assume a misunderstanding over the instructions they'd received.

After closing the garage he made a quick survey of the cottage and satisfied himself that it was as he had left it the previous night. The curtains were just as he remembered leaving them, and it was apparent that there had been no visitors in the course of the day.

Abruptly he turned his back on the cottage and walked down the short path and out into the lane. There wasn't another house within a quarter of a mile and he began to whistle softly. It was the contented whistle of a man who feels he has done a good job of work and is entitled to relax. He even enjoyed the two-mile walk to the main road, and was happy not to see a soul on his way.

His luck continued when the first lorry to come along stopped and gave him a ride. Just in case, he told the driver that he was on his way from Bristol and making for Kingston. This after he had learnt that the lorry was headed for the opposite side of London. He left it at one of the roundabouts on Western Avenue and had a further two-mile walk home.

It was five o'clock before he got into bed, and he then stayed there for the next twelve hours.

Not since God created the world had anyone accomplished so much in seven days, he reflected complacently as he drifted away into sleep.

6

He awoke with a start and a pervading feeling of unease which
he couldn't at first identify. It had something to do with Goodwin's car, and then it suddenly came to him. Supposing it was
stolen; that someone's mischievous interest in the obviously
deserted cottage took them up the path to its front-door and on
to the garage. And there they'd not only find the inviting key,
but inside, the car ready to be driven away. And, to make matters
worse, he now recalled that there was an approved school in the
area from which boys were frequently cutting loose to enjoy a
few days' wild depredation before being apprehended and returned to start all over again. Or so many of the local inhabitants
believed. What a fool he had been to have left the key in the
lock! Anywhere would have been better, it now seemed, as
he lay on his back frowning up at the ceiling.

It had been a shock to discover how many small details he had
failed to think of in advance. But were there any others? In his
mind he went over the events of Friday and Saturday nights.
No, apart from the minor mishaps which he had had to cope with,
he felt satisfied that he had committed no major mistakes which
might set off any alarm bells. It was a dent in his self-confidence,
however, even to have to consider that there might be some un-
thought-of point waiting to creep up and crack him over the
head from behind. He had planned every detail with such care
and overlooked nothing—or so he had thought until he had
come to put the car away.

He sprang from the bed. This was not the moment for
morbid hindthought. He'd just accomplished single-handed the
most audacious crime of the decade, possibly of the century,
with the prospect of becoming a rich man for the rest of his life.
He was already six thousand pounds up, and in a few weeks'

time he expected to be able to slide nearly a quarter of a million pounds his way. It would soon be time to begin the detailed planning of the next steps, those which would enable him to lay hold of Goodwin's entire estate. He wondered idly how many more times he would have to forge the dead man's signature before all the fruit was shaken from the tree; also whom he'd be depriving, apart from the Chancellor of the Exchequer. He had never heard Goodwin mention any family, but presumably he had some heirs somewhere. Too bad for them. By the time they did discover that Uncle or Cousin Geoffrey was dead, there'd be nothing left. His fat estate, together with someone called Colin Wise, would have vanished as completely as a trail of vapour.

Exhilarated by these potent thoughts, he shaved and set about sprucing himself up to go out. He put on the cardigan Miss Comber had given him and a sage green jacket which he had bought recently. A cup of coffee was all he wanted by way of nourishment, and, thus fortified, he locked the flat and walked off up the road with the easy assurance of a young man who feels the world is his oyster.

"Is that you, Peter boy?" Patrick Fox asked as he opened his front door.

"Right first time."

"I've come to know your knock."

Wise frowned. He didn't like to think that he could give himself away so easily, not even to an old blind man with heightened aural perception. He followed Fox into the back parlour, saw that there were no letters for Peter Fox and sat down.

"I thought you might drop in this evening, Peter boy."

"I don't usually on Sundays," Wise said sharply.

"True, but I still felt in my bones you would today." He grinned, showing an expanse of pale gum. "And I was right, Peter boy," he added triumphantly. "You have come." He rubbed his hands together with the dry parchment sound which always slightly repelled Wise. "Had a busy week, Peter boy?"

"Average."

Fox's grey, cloudy eyes peered in Wise's direction with puzzled curiosity. "You all right, Peter boy?"

"Sure, fine."

"You don't sound yourself."

"I'm fine." He hesitated. "There is one thing I ought to mention, Patrick." The old man leant forward, his expression attentive but wholly impassive. "It's just possible that . . . er . . . someone may come here making inquiries about me. It's very unlikely, I think, but . . . er . . . just possible."

"Yes, Peter boy?"

"Well, that's really all," Wise said uneasily.

There was a few seconds' silence before Fox spoke. "That's all right then, isn't it, Peter boy? I can't tell anyone more than I know, whoever it is. I can only tell them that Peter Fox is my friend, and if they want to know more about him they must knock on another door."

"Thanks, Patrick," Wise said, and meant it. He felt somehow that another link had been forged in their curious, unquestioning friendship. "Shall I read to you for a bit? I've brought *The News of the World* with me."

Fox sniffed. "I used to like that paper when it had reports of all the murder cases every week. It was good in those days." He shook his head sorrowfully. "Now it's all sex." An impish grin lit up his face. "And I'm past sex now, Peter boy, though I still like a good murder."

"I'll see what I can find," Wise said equably. Much as he liked Fox, he had no intention of gratifying his yearning for a good murder from his own personal record book. He scanned the pages. "Here's a piece about a woman who tried to poison her husband by slipping arsenic into his cup of early morning tea."

"What a mean trick," Fox remarked with interest. "Why'd she do it?"

"She was in love with the lodger."

"Oh, that old lark."

"Except that in this case he was her father-in-law."

"Disgusting! The bitch deserves all she gets. I'd give her five years."

"She didn't actually harm him. He spat out the tea as soon as he tasted it."

"I'd give her another five for being a bungler. I've no patience with the incompetence of some murderers these days." Wise smiled, but ceased abruptly as Fox went on, "Why are you smiling, Peter boy?"

"How the hell did you know I was smiling?"

Fox chuckled. "You get to sense all sorts of things when you're blind. Why were you?"

"Oh, just the way you were referring to murderers as though they were the same as bus drivers, lawyers or television repair men, some better than others."

"Well, it's so. And the most efficient of them all one never hears of."

Wise decided it was time to take the old man's mind off a topic so close to home, however tempting it was to play along with him. Patrick was too sharp, and sooner or later he would discern something he was not meant to. Wise turned determinedly to the sports page.

After leaving Fox, he caught a bus up to the West End. It was late March, and there was sudden definite promise of spring in the warm, balmy air. Three days before, people had gasped and lowered their heads in defence as they were met round every corner by a blast of biting wind. But this evening they were strolling, with muscles relaxed, in a mood to enjoy nature's unexpected offering and hoping it wasn't going to be capriciously whisked away.

Wise left the bus at Hyde Park Corner and walked along Piccadilly. Along the north side where the motor showrooms were. He stopped at the first and, hands thrust deep into his pockets, gazed at a bright red sports coupé which filled the window. It was a real beauty, anyone could see that. There was nothing cheap about it, and it would still look good even if you switched off the demonstration lights and sprayed it with wet mud.

Other people also stopped to gaze and then moved on again, but Wise remained standing squarely in front of the window with an expression of devouring absorption, unaware of the nudges and occasional giggles which his presence evoked.

Cars such as this one didn't bear price tickets, but—and this was better than all the spring evenings put together—he could afford to buy it whenever he wanted.

He was about to move on when he caught sight of his reflection in the plate glass and gave himself the faintest of winks.

Further along the road, he stopped to look into other show-room windows, but nothing else interested him any more. He surveyed their contents with indifference bordering on contempt. These cars might be all right for the masses, for seedy clerks with dreary wives and charmless children, for retired civil servants, for the hordes of unsuccessful business representatives who cluttered up the roads seven days a week. It was all they deserved, anyway.

Just before he reached Piccadilly Circus he turned down into St. James's and made a round of the art gallery windows in that district. But he found nothing to take his fancy. There were pictures of four-masted sailing ships on boisterous seas, of lovely sand dunes and lowering skies, of Constable landscapes and of Landseer squires with their adoring dogs—the sort of pictures which in Colin Wise's view were bought by those with more money than artistic imagination. He recrossed Piccadilly and walked up Bond Street. In one of the first windows he stopped in front of there was a picture which seized his attention in the same way as the red coupé had done. It looked as though it had been painted on top of a hill. There was green forest in the fore-ground giving way to blue sea. But it was the colours rather than the composition which held him spellbound. Various shades of green and blue melting into each other with the appearance of richest shot silk. He suddenly saw himself sprawled in a chair in his new home just gazing at this picture hour upon hour. He longed to possess it. He didn't know who had painted it— he didn't care. It was obviously someone with exceptional feeling for colour. It didn't need the hallmark of a Bond Street setting to proclaim its quality; one would have recognised that if it had been hanging on the steamy wall of a works canteen.

He made a note of the name of the gallery, and, feeling pleasantly elated, started for home. He had no desire to mingle further with the crowds, and the thought of fighting for a snack in some chromium establishment reeking of onion and cheap cooking oil was utterly repellent. Soon he would know those places only from the outside. He didn't suppose he'd have any difficulty becoming acclimatised to the sort of restaurants his new wealth would lead him to. Not that he intended to guzzle away a fortune, but it would be pleasant to enter the most famous eating portals when he was in the mood.

He had been out of his bed only six hours when he returned to it, relaxed and contented. His last lazy thought was of where Goodwin's plane had reached by now. Perhaps it was already in Australia. Faithful Hilda for certain would be picturing her master surrounded by kangaroos and koala bears. Only B.O.A.C. and Colin Wise knew different, and only one of them the truth. Snug in the possession of his secret, he curled up into a foetus and fell asleep.

7

Wise felt that the next few days were going to be a bore. His plans had reached the stage of a cook who has made her cake and put it in the oven to bake and has nothing more to do until the time arrives to take it out. All that's permissible is the occasional glance to ensure it hasn't blown its top, and some wouldn't even recommend this.

However, since one of his Monday-morning calls took him close to Goodwin's cottage, he seized the opportunity to drive past. There were a couple of windows open, and it was apparent that Hilda was somewhere inside, but it looked in every way the image of normality. He didn't quite know what he had expected to find—a posse of police digging up the garden?—but it was reassuring to observe the complete absence of any untowardness.

It was also not far out of his way to pass by the field of old oil drums. He smiled slightly as he reflected on the subtlety of that choice. As he turned down the lane towards the field he saw a youth standing outside the entrance. The youth looked round and held up his hand to halt Wise. At the same moment a lorry swung out into the lane, and with a thumbs-up sign in Wise's direction the youth clambered into the cab and the vehicle roared away, the din of its exhaust drowned by the clatter of empty oil drums bouncing about inside.

Aghast at the implication of what he'd witnessed, Wise continued to stare after it until a hoot behind reminded him that he was stationary in the middle of the lane. He drove into the side, and when the car had passed followed it as far as the entrance to the field. He feared to turn his head and know the worst.

Supposing Goodwin's decomposing head was bouncing about in the back of that lorry! Supposing the drum containing it had fallen over and the contents had spilled out! Even though it might no longer be recognisable—it hardly could be after sixty hours—there'd be enough to indicate that these were no ordinary dregs. Slowly, and as though he were suffering from a painful neck, he turned his gaze into the field.

What on Friday night had been a high pyramid of drums was now a shambolic pile. Over half of them had been removed, and the remainder looked as though the ground had been pulled away from beneath them. While he was still gazing morosely in their direction, a man appeared in the gateway.

"What can I do for you?" he asked in a surly tone.

"Nothing, thanks. I just parked here to have a smoke."

"You're blocking the entrance. There's a lorry wants to get in."

Wise clenched the steering-wheel till it felt like a bone running through his hand.

"Taking away the rest of those drums?" he asked in a tight voice.

"No, them old tyres in the far corner." The man's eyes glinted hopefully. "Are you interested, by any chance, in making an offer for the rest of them drums? There are still around twelve dozen there."

" 'Fraid I wouldn't know what to do with that number." A sudden idea entered his head. "Would you be interested in selling just a few, say half a dozen?"

"Might do."

"May I go and take a look?"

"Go ahead, but get your van out of the way first."

Wise drove on a few yards, then walked across to the scattered pile of drums. They were alike except that some bore more dents and scars than others. There was nothing in particular to distinguish the one in which he'd hidden Goodwin's head, but he did remember roughly where he had put it.

For the benefit of the men loading the lorry on the other side of the field, he pretended to be making a close examination of individual drums. Except that there wasn't all that much pretence about it, for he poked amongst them with all the earnestness of a geologist examining a mound of prehistoric flints.

Suddenly he espied it at the back and was horrified to notice in daylight that it was distinguishable from most of those around it by a cut at the top which he had made to get the head in. He felt sick at the proximity of disaster, the imminent torpedoing of all his careful plans, for even when a torpedo has been spotted it still has to be deflected from its lethal course.

He became aware that the men had finished what they were doing and were looking in his direction. The surly one began walking over and Wise hastened to head him off.

"I'd like to buy half a dozen," he said breathlessly as they came up to each other.

"O.K."

"How much?"

"Say a quid." Wise handed him a pound note. "Take your pick. We're just off." He grinned slyly. "Nobody'd be any the wiser if you took seven. But no more than that, mind you," he added, threateningly.

Wise watched the lorry depart before driving Mr. Gracey's van into the field and loading it, as he'd been invited to do, with seven drums. Six of them, he thought, would make a nice present for Mr. Gracey, who was always complaining about the lack of waste containers.

"I bought these for you, Mr. Gracey," he would say with modest pride. "I thought they'd come in useful." No, not "bought", but "scrounged". He'd never yet bought his employer a present, and it might be inviting suspicion to reveal that he had actually paid money for the drums. Meanwhile, however, he had to get rid of the seventh.

From a quick glance into its murky interior he had seen that the acid had completed its major work and that, even if teeth and bone still remained, all skin and tissue and hair had been converted into a disgusting oily residue, such as no one would be greatly surprised to find in an old oil drum.

There was a rash of disused gravel pits in the area, all filled with water, which, he'd been told, was up to fifteen feet deep in parts, and one of these seemed to provide the best available resting-place for Goodwin's disturbed remains.

He knew the pits attracted a number of anglers at weekends, but he reckoned they should be deserted in the middle of a working day. Moreover, it wasn't school holidays, so they shouldn't be festering with children either. He didn't know what effect the acid would have on the fish and was too worried to mind, though he didn't want them floating dead on the surface as a result of his action. But this seemed unlikely, and, anyway, it was a risk he must accept in the abnormal circumstances.

There was a solitary youth fishing in the first pit he came to, and he drove on to another a couple of hundred yards down the lane. There was no one about, and its high banks of excavated material, running round the perimeter in a range of jagged hillocks, provided ideal concealment of his movements.

Holding the fateful drum away from his body, he scrambled down one of the hillocks and stood at the edge of the placid water. Then, adopting a throwing stance, he swung the drum to and fro by its handle, pendulum-like, to get the feel of it. It wasn't heavy, just cumbersome. At length he was ready and, taking a quick look around to make sure he was unwatched, made two practice swings, and the third time his arm came through he released the drum. It hit the water about thirty feet from the bank, where, to Wise's horrified gaze, it gently bobbed and showed no inclination to sink.

Although it listed, the open end was several inches above the water line, and in that position it might float for ever. Savagely Wise picked up a large stone and hurled it as if at a fairground Aunt Sally. He missed and with the next, too, but with his third and fourth shots he found his mark. The only result, however, was to drive his target a few yards farther out.

He looked about him desperately. There was nothing for it but to strip and swim. First, however, he scrambled to the top of the hillock to make sure he wasn't likely to be interrupted. An empty landscape met his gaze. Returning to the edge of the pit, he took off all his clothes except for his underpants and entered the water.

It was colder than anything he had ever known, but there was no time for customary by-play and he waded in. Within two yards he was up to his shoulders and he began to swim a laborious breast-stroke towards the taunting object. At one point he thought he was going to develop cramp in his stomach, and his legs were so cold that he became unaware of them as belonging to his body. But somehow they managed to do as bidden by his brain and propel him forward.

When at last he reached the drum he held it at arms' length, and with his hands clamped to its sides pulled it under. There was a noise like a giant swallowing a gallon of beer as he thrust it away from him and swam furiously for the bank. Teeth chattering and trembling all over, he climbed out and looked back. No sign of the drum remained, only a faint scumminess where it had been. At this moment, however, he was almost past caring. The combined physical and mental ordeal had—temporarily—numbed his zest to survive. If a squad of policemen had appeared over the top of the hillock he'd have crumpled weeping into their arms.

Using his vest as a towel, he mopped at his frozen limbs and got dressed as quickly as he could. By the time he had regained the van and lit a cigarette his confidence was beginning to reassert itself. He even managed a rueful smile as he recalled a line he'd learnt at school about adversity not being without comforts and hopes. He couldn't remember who had written it, only that the particular poet had seemed a bit hipped on adversity, but it was a line his mind had hung on to—one which had given him its own comfort and hope from time to time.

With the van heater switched full on, he slowly thawed out as he drove back to the shop. Mr. Gracey accepted the drums with restrained gratitude after Wise had explained that he had acquired them from a garage friend who'd been about to throw them away.

"They only need a bit of a clean out and they'll come in useful," he said encouragingly.

"Leave 'em outside in the yard for the present," Mr. Gracey had replied, in a tone which lacked enthusiasm.

It was getting on towards the end of the afternoon and he and Mr. Gracey were completing a repair job in the workshop when Mrs. Gracey suddenly appeared. This in itself was a rare enough occurrence, as normally she transmitted all her information and requirements through the intercom. which had been rigged up between the front and rear premises. She was carrying an evening paper, and the inevitable cigarette stuck out of the side of her mouth. One hand clasped an orange cardigan across her neck.

"Good thing I sent Mr. Goodwin his account," she declared, gesturing with the newspaper. "There's a bit about him here."

Wise wanted to snatch the paper from her, tell her she must be talking nonsense. How could there yet be anything in the paper about him? Why, it was only a few hours ago he had passed Goodwin's cottage and seen that normality reigned. How dare she startle him with oblique observations.

"What?" Mr. Gracey asked with only mild interest.

"You can read it for yourselves. I think I hear someone in the shop." She threw the paper down and tripped out. Then, popping her head back through the door, she added, "He paid it, too. His cheque was in Saturday's post. Perhaps we ought to tell the police."

Mr. Gracey and Wise exchanged bewildered glances. "Have a look and find out what she's talking about," Mr. Gracey said in a resigned tone.

Wise picked up the paper as though it might be radioactive and with mounting anxiety turned its pages. He had reached the centre before a headline leapt out at him.

"Author Mystery", he read, and beneath this a report which ran: "It is understood that the police have been called in to solve the mystery surrounding Bucks author Mr. Geoffrey Goodwin's departure for Australia on Saturday afternoon. The only thing known is that Mr. Goodwin didn't leave on his scheduled flight. This afternoon a police spokesman said, 'Mrs. Hilda Paget, who is Mr. Goodwin's housekeeper, got in touch with us and we are making inquiries.' The spokesman declined to comment further."

"Well, go on, read it out," Mr. Gracey said testily as Wise continued to stare glassily at the paragraph.

He did so in a constricted voice, which mercifully Mr. Gracey seemed not to notice. When he had finished Mr. Gracey turned back to his work bench.

"What do you think's happened?" he asked, in an absent voice.

Wise shrugged. "Don't know. Sounds odd, doesn't it?"

8

It had required considerable effort on Wise's part to hide the concern which the newspaper report had caused him. He felt like a householder whose attention has been drawn to a small crack in a newly-plastered ceiling. Will it stop there or is it only a matter of time before it widens and perhaps the whole ceiling comes crashing down?

He was still trying to foresee the implications when he packed up to go home, and in his preoccupied state didn't notice Lesley Gracey standing over in a corner of the yard.

"Guess who?" said a voice behind him, and at the same moment a pair of hands were clasped over his eyes. Except that they didn't remain there but took the opportunity of caressing his face.

He released himself and swung round to find Lesley watching him with an eager, hopeful smile.

"Don't ever do that again. I don't like it."

It was as though he had given her a stinging slap across both cheeks. She turned bright red, her eyes filled with tears and her lower lip began to tremble.

"I'm sorry," he said gruffly, "but you startled me. My thoughts were elsewhere; and, anyway, I have a thing about people touching my face."

She appeared to study him in an effort to decide whether to accept or reject his less than meagre olive-branch, though there was never any doubt which it would be. "This is the week you said we'd fix an evening for me to visit you."

"Sorry, not this week, Lesley."

Her face fell. "There you go again, making excuses. If you don't do anything in the evenings, why can't I come? I promise I won't be a nuisance—and, anyway, you promised. . . ."

"You shall come, but not this week." They glared at each other in naked resentment: Wise because he realised he must provide some fresh plausible reason for putting her off, which at the same time would keep her docile. "I'm planning to repaint the kitchen, that's why I can't do any entertaining this week."

"I'd love to help you, Colin. May I?"

He shook his head. "Only just enough room for one person in my kitchen."

She looked at him doubtfully. "You're not still cross with me, are you?"

"No."

"Promise?"

"Promise."

"And you do . . . do like me?"

"I like you all right."

With a sudden dart forward she planted a kiss on the side of his chin and dashed off.

As if I didn't have enough on my mind, he thought, without being the target of a schoolgirl crush. And I'm not even flattered. . . .

All that evening he brooded over the latest disturbing development. At one point he had almost made up his mind to telephone Goodwin's housekeeper the next morning and see what he could find out. He knew that she liked him and felt sure she would tell him as much as she was able. Furthermore, the paragraph in the evening paper provided him with a perfectly legitimate reason to phone her and inquire what had happened. But supposing the police found out from her that he had called, wouldn't they regard it as rather odd? Generally speaking, television repair men don't make personal inquiries after their customers' well-being, that is, unless they happen to be on terms of friendship, and he certainly didn't wish the police to start probing in that direction. No, on second thoughts it would be wiser not to telephone. And on this negative and unsatisfactory note he went to bed.

Some time in the night he woke up with a hoarse shout and lay back exhausted on discovering he was still in his own bed. He had dreamt he was in the middle of a lake which was so large that its shores couldn't be seen, and that he was grappling with a huge barrel which refused to be sunk. It bobbed and tossed and slithered from him every time he fought to push it under.

The next morning he rose, feeling washed out and shivery. He reckoned he must have caught a chill, but this was no day to stay in bed. He had to keep going and appear normal, whatever his bodily sensations.

He left home earlier than usual and bought two newspapers on his way to work. One of them contained nothing at all about Goodwin, but the other ran quite a story. One of its reporters had obviously been rooting hopefully around but had little to file, save speculation. Wise, however, was disturbed to see that Hilda had refused to be drawn into making any comments, saying that she had been told not to.

Who had told her not to? The police? Goodwin's lawyer? And, anyway, what did she know that had to be kept from the public?

Wise stared absently out of the bus window. After reviewing his possible courses of action, he had decided that the only sensible one was to sit tight. He must certainly keep his ears open and his eyes skinned, but apart from that he would do nothing. Watch and wait would be his guiding motto.

Luckily, he had a busy day and little spare time to feed his mind with fanciful speculation. He was, moreover, able to keep out of Mr. Gracey's way and also avoided seeing Lesley.

It was around eight o'clock that Tuesday evening, when he was in the middle of his supper, that the door bell rang. It could only be Lesley and he didn't bother to peer first out of the living-room window before going down to open the door. One thing was certain: she wasn't coming in. She could have hysterics on the step, but she'd get no farther. His indignant determination grew with each stair he descended. This time he'd really see her off. He flung open the door. Two men stood there.

"Mr. Wise?" asked the taller. Wise felt his mouth sag open. "Could we come in and have a word with you? We're police officers."

9

Wise led the way upstairs and into the living-room. The two officers followed him in silence.

"Sorry to come worrying you at this hour of the evening," the taller one said pleasantly. "I'm Detective-Superintendent Manton of the Metropolitan Police, and this is Detective-Inspector Winslow of the Bucks Police." Manton looked round the room. "Mind if we sit down?"

"Go ahead." Wise was surprised to hear his own voice emerge naturally. He sat down without thinking in the chair Goodwin had occupied, and faced the officers over on the sofa. There was a quiet repose about Manton that he found at the same time reassuring and disconcerting—reassuring because he looked far removed from a bully, disconcerting because he seemed so full of easy confidence.

"Have you seen the newspapers today, Mr. Wise?" Manton asked in the same conversational tone.

"I've glanced at a couple."

"Read about Mr. Goodwin?"

"Yes, I was interested in that bit. I've been to his house. I used to look after his set."

Manton nodded as though this was some question-and-answer game proceeding the way all of them wanted. "As you've probably guessed, that's what we've come about. You may be able to help us. When did you last see him?"

The question was asked in a tone which implied Manton set no great store by the answer, but to Wise it was like a hook under the chin. He thought faster than he'd ever done before. Truth or untruth, that was the stark decision confronting him, and with no more than a few seconds to make up his mind.

"I saw him on Friday, the day before he was leaving for Australia."

"Did you call at his house that day, then?"

"No. As a matter of fact he came here."

Wise was certain he noticed a faint expression of disappointment pass across Inspector Winslow's face. If this was so, then he had obviously made the right decision. They must have evidence of Goodwin's visit on Friday night. This was going to be a real poker game, and now that his first shock had worn off he felt stimulated by the challenge to his wits.

Manton affected an expression of urbane surprise. "Mr. Goodwin come here? Did he often?"

"That was the only time."

"What was the reason for his visit?"

"He came to see some of my drawings. I'd told him about them and he said he'd like to look at them."

"But this was his last evening. Wasn't it a bit unusual to pay a social call of that sort?"

Wise shrugged. "All I can say is that he came."

"What time?"

"About half-past eight."

"How long did he stay?"

"Not much more than half an hour."

"And then?"

"He left. He had his car outside and he just drove off."

"Was that the last you saw of him?"

"Yes."

"He didn't come back or anything?"

Wise frowned. "No-o."

Manton shifted on the sofa. "To date, Mr. Wise, you're the last person to have seen him."

The two officers raised their heads and gazed at him like a pair of ravens.

Wise made a helpless face. "I'm afraid I still can't tell you any more."

"You may be able to," Manton said, with a wisp of a smile. "Let's see." He might have been encouraging a diffident child,

73

and Wise waited impassively but with all senses alerted. "Do you know anything about Mr. Goodwin's habits?"

"Such as?"

"Where he put his car keys when he wasn't driving?"

"I'm afraid not."

"Or where he kept his garage key, for example?"

"No idea."

So that was it. He'd drawn attention to something being wrong by leaving the keys as he had. And now he was being asked questions of the have-you-stopped-beating-your-wife order. Well, "no" was obviously the right answer. After all, who apart from Goodwin and his garage people should be expected to know his habits with the keys.

"Did he tell you details of his departure? Flight, time, things like that?"

"Only that he was leaving London Airport on Saturday afternoon."

"When he came here on Friday evening, did he mention any change of plan?"

"No."

"How did he appear to you that evening?"

Another of those questions which required lightning thought. They came in with the regularity of every seventh wave. How far should he go in suggesting that perhaps there was something a little different about Goodwin that evening, something which would help to explain a subsequent unusual pattern of behaviour?

"He seemed excited, except that it was more a sort of suppressed excitement. I thought it was because he was going off the next day, but, thinking back, I'm not so sure."

"Can you give us anything to go on? How did this 'sort of suppressed excitement' manifest itself?"

"It was in his eyes chiefly. They were particularly shiny as though he was about to spring a practical joke on someone." *Yes, that was rather a clever touch.*

Manton pursed his lips. "How much of this is being wise after the event?" he asked agreeably.

"I don't think any of it." Wise replied in a faintly reproachful tone.

Manton exchanged a whispered word with Inspector Winslow and they both stood up. Turning to Wise, he said, "I should very much like to see your drawings myself before we go. Could we do that?"

"I'll fetch them." So they didn't believe any drawings existed! He could barely refrain from grinning as he left the room.

"You did all these?" Manton asked in a tone from which surprise couldn't be concealed.

"All of them and a good many more."

"I'm no artist, but they look pretty good to me. What do you think, Inspector?"

Inspector Winslow nodded uncertainly, while Wise, watching them, enjoyed a moment of triumph.

"Nice place you've got here," Manton remarked, moving out into the hall and poking his head round the kitchen door. He subjected the bedroom and bathroom to similar careful scrutinies. At the top of the stairs, he turned, "Well, thank you for your help, Mr. Wise. We may have to bother you again. It depends."

"Have you any idea what's happened to Mr. Goodwin?" Wise asked, with what he hoped was the right degree of interest.

"At the moment we're completely in the dark. Personally" —he gave Wise and Inspector Winslow a wry smile—"I have a feeling it's one of these author's publicity stunts. Probably planned the whole thing, and just when the forces of six continents are on the look-out for him he'll pop up all cheerful and pretend to wonder what all the fuss is about."

Wise laughed. A laugh of considerable relief had they but known. "There is one question I'd like to ask you before you go."

"There's no charge for asking," Manton said, beginning to descend the stairs.

"What put you on to coming to see me?"

"Oh, that! Just that we happened to find directions how to get here in the glove pocket of Mr. Goodwin's car. Good night, Mr. Wise."

IO

The flat seemed different after the officers had departed. Wise was immediately aware of it as he moved restlessly from room to room. Somehow their presence had despoiled the atmosphere of "home" which was so precious to him. The urbane Superintendent Manton and the silent but watchful Inspector Winslow had managed to impart a sourness which now seemed to be reflected at him from every wall.

He couldn't get over the random stroke of fate which had led the police to his doorstep. It was just abominably unfair, though he kicked himself for having overlooked a search of the car's pockets. At some time or another Goodwin must have written down the directions Wise had given him and then put the piece of paper in the glove compartment for use on what was to be his last ride in the car.

Well, that little oversight might have brought Wise to the brink, but it was going to require a lot more to send him over it. Nevertheless, to think that but for a scruffy bit of paper he could just as well have been on another planet for all the police knew of his connection with the affair. And now . . .

As he prowled morosely about the flat, giving thought to possible counter-moves which were open to him, his fore-boding only increased. *He was the last person to have seen Goodwin alive*. That was, and would continue to be, the hard core of police suspicion. They would now watch him, check on his movements and generally expose him to an icy blast of their cold-war tactics, and all because of a bloody scrap of paper.

Well, he was as equally determined that their inquiries should encroach no further, that he would block every approach they tried to make, and that even if they continued to suspect him for months on end they'd have no hope of translating suspicion into certain knowledge.

He went into his bedroom and kicked off his shoes, putting on a pair of backless slippers. The thing he felt most bitter about was the abrupt vanishment of his prospects of harvesting the remainder of Goodwin's estate. But perhaps he was being unduly pessimistic and it was too early to write off all his hopes in that direction. Meanwhile, there *was* six thousand pounds in the bank which not even clever rozzers would be able to find.

This set his mind off on another tack. If the police suspected foul play, then obviously the first thing they would look for would be motive, and he, Wise, had none. None, that is, that they could possibly discover. So sooner or later they must conclude that Goodwin's disappearance and probable murder resulted from something out of his past. The settlement of an old score perhaps. He had travelled a lot and lived a pretty varied life, so there'd be a wide range of possibilities for them to delve into. They'd be at it for weeks and months, while he, Wise, would have to sit tight until the inquiry was called off— if not formally, at least in practice. But that didn't mean he would have to remain in Mr. Gracey's employ. Indeed, the sooner he found another job, the better. If the police were all that nosy, he didn't mind telling them of his intention. It might be an idea to do so, anyway, to show he hadn't anything to hide.

In the middle of the mental exercise of digging in and revetting his defences, the telephone rang. He lifted the receiver but didn't speak.

"Mr. Wise? Superintendent Manton here. Sorry to bother you again, but I'd like to come round for a few minutes."

"Now, do you mean?"

"Yes, just one or two further points I'd like to clear up."

"What's wrong with the phone?"

"I think it would be better if I came round," Manton replied smoothly. "Doesn't matter if you're in your pyjamas. We'll be with you in a quarter of an hour."

He rang off without waiting for further response, leaving Wise's mind to dwell uncomfortably on the reason for a second visit within a matter of two hours.

If they were proposing to arrest him, they'd hardly have announced their arrival. The calmer half of his mind pounced on the thought even as it was being formulated. What fanciful nonsense! How could they arrest him when they didn't even know what had happened to Goodwin? *This isn't like you, Colin Wise. Take a grip on yourself, boy. You've played it cool so far. Continue.*

When the front-door bell rang he went down and let the officers in with an indulgent smile as though they might be children who had come back for their galoshes.

Manton nodded and headed upstairs, followed by the dour inspector from Bucks. As Wise came into the living-room behind them, Manton swung round. "I understand you borrowed Mr. Gracey's van last Friday evening?"

"Mmm."

"To collect a chair, is that right?"

"Yes."

"But this was the evening you were expecting a visitor?"

"True," Wise answered quietly and met Manton's thoughtful gaze.

"Which chair?" His eyes went quickly round the room.

"One in my bedroom, if you want to know."

"May I see it?"

"Go ahead, you know the way."

They were obviously put out by their failure to disconcert him, and Wise was quick enough to realise this and relish the fact that he had the upper-hand. The business of the chair was something he had well buttoned up.

"That one?" Manton asked, pointing at a small wing-chair by the window. Wise nodded. It was one he had bought in a sale about three weeks before and Goodwin was the first person ever to have seen it in his home and he probably hadn't even noticed it. It had been sitting there waiting for this moment. Inspector Winslow walked across the room and gave it a closer scrutiny. Wise wondered what on earth he expected to learn.

"Where did you buy it?"

"In a sale."

"What sale? I'd like to have the address you went to to fetch it, Mr. Wise."

78

"Auckland Farm, near Heston." It was difficult not to let a slight crow creep into his voice, but that would be a mistake. No point in antagonising the police unless it would serve a purpose. He knew they were liable to react sharply if they reckoned someone was behaving too cockily. They didn't, as a breed, like being out-smarted, and were apt to have memories longer than an elephant's.

"And you attended a sale there on Friday night?"

"No. The sale was some time before. Perhaps I'd better explain. I bought that chair about two weeks ago, but I couldn't bring it away with me, so I left it in an outbuilding till I was able to fetch it, which was last Friday."

There was a silence while the two officers pondered. Wise himself also became thoughtful. It wasn't such a very convincing story heard aloud, even though they mightn't be able to disprove it. It was true he had bought the chair in a sale of furniture at Auckland Farm, but he'd brought it home the same day. Since, however, he knew the farm had been untenanted since then, no one could give the lie to his story.

"Of all evenings, last Friday seems a very curious one to have gone off on this errand." Wise remained impassive under Manton's gaze. "Why couldn't you have fetched it before?"

"It was a question of choosing the right moment to ask Mr. Gracey if I could borrow the van. He doesn't really like lending it to me."

"Why should the van have got so dirty fetching a chair?" Manton asked after another pause.

The old bastard really had been opening his mouth, Wise reflected grimly. In a patient tone he said, "I explained that to Mr. Gracey. I had to turn in a muddy lane."

"That wouldn't have made the interior dirty."

"It didn't."

"But you gave that a thorough washing, too, the next morning."

"True. Mr. Gracey had been good enough to lend me the van, so while I was at it I decided to make a good job at cleaning it. It was," he added with faint bite, "a way of saying a practical thank-you."

"I see," Manton remarked in a non-committal tone. "And what time did you get back here from fetching the chair?"

Wise thought rapidly. No one could possibly know that Goodwin had phoned him around half-past seven, and therefore, though it had the smell of a trap question, he felt safe in telling a straight-forward lie.

"I was away less than half an hour and was back just before eight."

"Did you stop anywhere on the way?"

"No."

"Is there anyone who can corroborate what you say?"

"Not that I know of."

"And was that the only journey you made in the van that evening?"

"Yes."

"And yet by the time you returned it the next morning you'd driven over sixty miles."

"I hadn't."

"Mr. Gracey says——"

"Mr. Gracey's mistaken," Wise broke in firmly. "I told him so at the time. He misread the clock."

"He doesn't think he did."

Wise shrugged. "I'm ready to have my sight tested against Mr. Gracey's any day you name. Anyway, what's the suggestion behind all these questions?"

Manton met his gaze and looked away. "No suggestions at all, Mr. Wise," he said peaceably. "Simply that we're investigating the disappearance of a man last known to have been in your company, and obviously we have to ask a lot of questions —as much, I'm sure, in your interest as anyone's."

Wise pretended to look mollified and Manton made to go. "If anything further occurs to you which could help our inquiries get in touch with me, won't you?"

"Certainly."

The two officers were crossing the yard when Manton looked toward the wide garage doors. "What do you keep in there?"

"Nothing, apart from old junk."

"Could we have a look?"

"I'll fetch the key, it's upstairs." Damn them for their cool impudence, Wise reflected, as he returned with it.

He opened the doors and switched on the light.

"Wonder you don't let it," Manton remarked conversationally as he peered around.

"I prefer not to."

"Don't blame you really. Worse than having a lodger in some ways. And right beneath your bedroom, too." He studied the floor. "Are those car marks?"

Wise followed his line of gaze and suddenly froze, for the wheel marks he saw had not just been made by *a* car, they'd been made by Goodwin's car.

"I put Mr. Gracey's van in here when I borrow it," he said dully.

"Yes, of course." Manton wandered over to a corner where there was a pile of cartons and various pieces of luggage. Wise watched him poke amongst them with a casual air. He seemed satisfied that none of them contained any arcane secrets and made to leave the garage. Wise saw him throw Inspector Winslow a small helpless smile.

"We'll say good night once again, Mr. Wise."

The inspector gave a curt nod in Wise's direction and followed Manton out to the car. Wise waited till they were out of sight before fetching a bucket of water and a broom amd setting to work on the garage floor.

If they had it in mind to return the next day and take measurements of wheel bases, they would be disappointed.

Moreover, his spirits rose with the very vigour of his scrubbing. It was the fact of doing something positive, of launching a sturdy counter-move against the enemy.

II

Mr. Gracey had already arrived and opened up the workshop when Wise appeared the next morning.

"'Morning, Colin," he said, with what Wise took to be nervous affability. Well, if he thought he was going to avoid trouble simply by saying good morning with greater warmth than usual he could start thinking again—and now.

"What've you been telling the police about me?" Wise's tone was as accusatorial as he could make it, and he was pleased to see Mr. Gracey flush.

"I only answered the questions they asked me," he said defensively.

"Like hell. You mean you sowed in their minds all sorts of doubts about what I was up to on Friday night."

"I certainly never——"

But Wise was not to be interrupted. "Did you have to tell them I washed the van so as to make it sound that I had something to hide? Also suggesting that I lied to you about the mileage? What did you want to do, have me arrested?"

"'Course I didn't," Mr. Gracey replied with spirit. "And, anyway, the van had done over sixty miles by the time you brought it back. I didn't misread the figures."

"You didn't misread the figures!" Wise ground out. "Why, you couldn't read your own name in letters six feet high!" He glared at his employer, compressing his lips tightly as if to hold back the dammed-up tide of recrimination which was waiting to pour forth. "What've I ever done to you, I'd like to know?"

"I——"

"I've worked hard, kept extra hours, brought you fresh business; and all for what? For you to suggest to the police at the first opportunity that I've been up to something criminal."

"I didn't. . . ."

"It's the bloody unfairness of it, that's what gets me," he concluded bitterly.

"I don't know what you're so upset about——"

"I'm upset because I don't like being put under a police microscope any more than anyone else."

"That's not my fault."

"You started them off."

"Now look here, Colin, I did no more than you'd have done in my position, and I certainly never suggested that you'd been up to anything you shouldn't have been."

"Oh, it's fine your saying this now," Wise jeered. "Anyway, you'd better start looking out for a new assistant."

"You're not leaving me?"

"Are you crazy? I don't work my guts out for employers who try and shop me with the police."

"When are you proposing to go?"

Wise ostentatiously studied his watch. "In about a couple of minutes' time."

"You can't. I'm entitled to a week's notice."

A chilly smile crept over Wise's features. "So you are. Know what you can do about it? Go running to those police you're so pally with."

He turned and walked out of the workshop, leaving Mr. Gracey staring stonily after him. He walked up to the main road and entered a café he frequently patronised, and, ordering a cup of coffee, went and sat over at a corner table by himself.

So now he was Colin Wise, unemployed. The absurd part was he hadn't really intended to hand in his notice. He had become carried away on the tide of his own indignation. Mr. Gracey had merely been the convenient focal point of his mounting resentment at all the things which had gone wrong in the last few days, culminating in the highly unwelcome intrusion of the police.

As the first remedial effects of his outburst began to wear off, he realised ruefully how ill-judged it had been. And, what was worse, it was so out of character. He, who almost made a fetish of self-containment, had allowed himself to be needled into a

83

display of uncontrolled emotion. Except that this wasn't quite true. The quarrel was of his contrivance, he had determined to excoriate his employer, but he had carried himself away. Having deliberately worked himself up, the dialogue had swerved off course and here he was without a job. Well, there was a lesson to be learnt there. But now what?

It wouldn't be long before the police learnt he had left Mr. Gracey's employ and that would certainly bring them post-haste round to the flat. They'd probably even expect to find him in the act of decamping, since, as related by Mr. Gracey, the mode of his departure would sound like a pretext for such a move. Except there again they would surely realise that if he really intended to disappear, he wouldn't be likely to proclaim it so crudely.

However, the point was that they wouldn't find him about to flit, and he would explain with dignity why he'd decided it was impossible to continue working for Mr. Gracey. It would be as well if he found another job immediately, as this would re-assure them about his motives.

He finished his coffee and left. The best thing he could do today, however, would be to return home and spend the time in some innocent domestic activity. He'd be available to all who came scurrying round to find out what he was up to. They'd be confronted by someone immured behind a wall of shock-proof self-control. Someone who had six thousand pounds safely tucked away in a hidden bank account.

He spotted the patrolling constable soon after he had turned down the road which led to his home. The man, who was about his own age, was on the opposite side of the road and made a not very expert attempt at masking his interest in Wise's approach. So old Gracey had already alerted them. It made Wise wonder if he hadn't been working for a professional informer all these months.

As soon as he was inside the flat he went and looked out of the lounge window and was not surprised to see that the officer had disappeared. Nor five minutes later to receive a telephone call from Superintendent Manton.

"I hear you've thrown in your job at Mr. Gracey's?"

84

"Yes."

"Not thinking of leaving the district, are you?"

"No."

"What made you quit so suddenly?"

"I should have thought you could have guessed."

"I never guess if I can get the information first hand."

"I don't care to go on working for someone who tries to put me in bad with the police."

"Aren't you being a little sensitive?"

"I don't think so. And what anyone else thinks doesn't matter."

"Are you proposing to take another job?"

"Yes."

"Soon?"

"Yes."

"Keep in touch with me, won't you?"

"I've already said I will."

"That's fine, then. 'Bye."

Shortly after the conversation was over, Wise noticed that the constable was back in the street. Presumably they intended to keep him under surveillance. Well, he hoped they'd enjoy themselves. He glanced up at the sky and smiled. There was going to be a heavy shower any minute now. Meanwhile, he decided to give the flat a good spring-clean, and went and climbed into his oldest pair of slacks and a well-frayed shirt, which he kept for messy jobs about the home.

From time to time he broke from his labours for a cup of coffee and a cigarette, but otherwise engrossed himself so that the hours ticked by, with his being hardly aware of the clock. It was around mid-afternoon when the front-door bell suddenly rang. From the lounge window he could see a familiarly shaped car parked outside. He went down expecting to find Manton, but was greeted by two strange faces.

"I'm Detective-Sergeant Chester," said the older man. He had a tough, battered look about him and a figure which told of heavy beer drinking. "And this is Detective-Constable Brook." Wise glanced at the other officer. He was considerably younger, had a grave expression and a pale complexion, and looked less

like a detective than an insurance clerk. "Detective-Superintendent Manton sent us along," Sergeant Chester continued.
"You don't have to agree to this, of course, but we'd like to take
a look round your place."

"I've no objection," Wise replied equably. "Any particular
purpose?"

"No, just a look around," Sergeant Chester answered in a
tone of off-hand rudeness. "We'll start down here. Can you
unlock the garage?" When Wise had done so, Chester said,
"We needn't keep you, you can get on with what you were
doing."

Colin Wise returned upstairs. He didn't care for Sergeant
Chester, who seemed to belong more to the secret police and who,
he guessed, would welcome the opportunities afforded by any
recalcitrant customers. He didn't envy Detective-Constable
Brook, but that was his look-out.

He was beginning to wonder how much longer they were
going to spend in the garage when he heard sounds out in the
yard. Peeping out of the window, he saw them bent over the
main drain into which flowed all the waste-pipes in the flat.
Sergeant Chester was prodding away with a stick. He said something to D.-C. Brook, who gave him an unhappy look before
rolling up one of his sleeves and plunging his arm into the drain
as far as it would go. His hand came up empty and he glanced
around for something to wipe it on.

Shortly after this, Wise heard them coming upstairs.

"Have you given the garage a clean since Mr. Manton was
here?"

"Yes."

"Why?"

"I'm in the process of giving the whole place a spring-clean."

Sergeant Chester grunted and disappeared into the bathroom,
followed by Brook, who, Wise felt, wasn't much enjoying himself.

Their search was thorough and complete, though, to give
them credit, they did, as they moved from room to room, restore
everything as they found it. Every cupboard and every drawer
was opened; every corner was examined. As he watched them,

Wise congratulated himself on his equal thoroughness in having disposed of every single trace of Goodwin. And that before he ever expected to have the police taking his home apart.

"Anything above?" Sergeant Chester asked curtly, casting his glance at the ceiling. "Is there an attic up there?"

"No. You've seen the lot."

Sergeant Chester stuck out his lower lip and stared sourly about him, while Wise and D.-C. Brook awaited his pleasure.

"Come on," he said, turning to his companion, "there's nothing further to be done here." His tone matched his expression in disgruntlement, and without a further word or glance at Wise he set off down the stairs. Wise heard the front door close and went and watched their departure from the window. He wondered with how much more of that sort of treatment he'd have to put up. Never mind, he was now prepared and able to cope with whatever came. He returned to the kitchen where he had been interrupted in the act of cleaning the gas stove.

By the time he had finished he felt in need of a bath, not only to wash off the dirt but to relax himself after the nervous tensions of the day. As he lay luxuriating in the water which was as hot as he could bear it, his eye alighted on the scratch marks, and he ran his finger over their surface wondering if there was anything he could do about them.

It was almost at this same moment that Detective-Sergeant Chester was reporting to Manton. "Not a sausage, sir, except for some score marks in the bath which looked of recent origin. D.-C. Brook photographed them."

"Does Wise know?"

Sergeant Chester shook his head. "He never even saw the camera. Brook kept it out of sight."

"And you didn't ask him about the marks?"

"No, sir."

"Good. We'll let him think they haven't been noticed. And, anyway, by themselves they're evidence of nothing."

Wise soaked until he felt faintly sick, then got out and carefully dried himself. He couldn't bear putting on his clothes so long as any moisture remained on his body. When he was dressed, he grilled himself two lamb chops and tomatoes and finished off his meal with cheese. He had just completed the washing-up when the door-bell rang. A quick look through the window revealed no sign of a car—the police watchdog who on and off throughout the day had been patrolling outside had also disappeared—and his visitor was standing so close to the door that whoever it was couldn't be seen. He ran down and opened it, to be confronted by a thoroughly scared-looking Lesley Gracey.

For several seconds they stared at each other in complete silence. While he tried to make up his mind what line to adopt, she watched him with anxious eyes.

"You'd better come in," he said at length in a neutral tone. She stepped past him and mounted the stairs. "Last door on the right," he directed her at the top. As she preceded him along the passage, he noticed how eagerly she peered into the rooms on either side.

"What a lovely room!" she exclaimed with bright-eyed pleasure as she stood in the middle of the lounge. "It's my ideal, Colin."

"Before you go any further with that, you'd better tell why you're here."

Her expression became anguished. "Can't you guess?" Then in a sudden rush: "We can go on seeing each other, can't we, Colin, even though you're not working for Daddy any more?"

He gestured impatiently. "How much do you know, Lesley? Did your father tell you why I'd slung the job?"

"He just said there'd been some trouble between you and you'd walked out," she said in a frightened voice.

"He didn't say what sort of trouble?"

She shook her head. "It's nothing serious, is it?"

"Once people start stirring things up, one never knows," he remarked darkly.

"Please let me help you, Colin. I'll do anything you ask me."

He looked thoughtfully at her. Perhaps he'd take her up on that offer, but not yet. The time might come when he would be glad to call upon an ally, particularly one who would undoubtedly do exactly as she was bidden. But there would be dangers in embroiling her too soon or, rather, until necessity demanded.

For the time being he was still playing the indignant innocent who had nothing to hide and nothing to fear, and certainly no need at this stage of a concocted alibi.

His face broke into a smile. "I believe you would, too," he said lightly, touching the tip of her nose with his finger, "but I don't need any help at the moment. Thanks all the same, Lesley."

He realised that the silly kid was thrilled at the remotely dangled prospect of being called upon to help him, and he would certainly feel no compunction about making use of her.

"Shall I show you the rest of the flat?" he asked cheerfully.

"Mm, I'd love to see it."

They finished their tour in the kitchen, where Wise, eagerly assisted by Lesley, made some coffee. The girl was obviously in a seventh heaven of delight.

"And to think," she said suddenly, "how terrified I was while I was waiting for you to answer the door. I thought you might be furious, and yet I had to come."

"You must promise me one thing, Lesley," he said seriously.

"Anything."

"That you won't come again without first phoning to find out if it's all right."

Her face momentarily clouded, then cleared. "I promise."

"And you'd better not tell your parents, either, that you've been here."

"I shan't. They think I've gone to the cinema with Barbara."

He walked up to the main road with her and waited till a bus came. She blew him a kiss as it drew away from the kerb, and he answered with a flip of the hand.

Quite a profitable evening, he reflected as he returned home. The day which had begun badly and become worse had ended, after all, on an upward note.

12

During the next few days Wise found a new job—a temporary one with a large firm, which suited him admirably—and generally went about his business as though he hadn't a care in the world. He bought rather more newspapers than usual, but beyond an occasional short paragraph saying that author Geoffrey Goodwin's mysterious disappearance was still being investigated there was nothing to disturb his restored confidence, which reflected the old adage about half a loaf being better than no bread at all.

There was, however, one matter over which he worried, and this concerned Patrick Fox. He thought it extremely probable that the police or Goodwin's own solicitors would have got on to the cheque for six thousand pounds drawn in favour of Peter Fox. He didn't know how much information about their client the Shepherd's Bush branch of the United Bank would vouch-safe, though his address would be about all they could tell anyone, and this would automatically lead the inquiry to his old blind friend.

He yearned to know whether in fact the police had been to see Patrick Fox and, if so, what he had told them. He realised, however, that they could well be keeping Fox's house under observation, not to mention the intermittent watch on himself, and in these circumstances any attempt to visit his friend could be the most fatal thing for him to do. It would be akin to scaling the eyes of the police. He'd just have to cut Fox out of his life for the time being and hope the old man would understand.

He had just returned home at the end of his third day in his new job when the telephone rang. He had neither changed nor eaten, and was feeling in no mood to be pushed around.

"Superintendent Manton here, Mr. Wise. I'd like you to come round to the station for a few minutes. I'll send a car for you straight away, if that'll be all right."

"I've only just walked in and I haven't had a meal yet."

"We shan't keep you long."

"What's it all about?"

"I'll tell you when you get here."

"Surely you can give me half an hour, I'm hungry."

"All right. You'll find the car waiting outside. Don't be too long."

Manton rang off, and a few minutes later a car drew up in the road outside. Wise could see two figures in the front. They lit cigarettes and sat back to wait for him. Wise went into the kitchen, but found his appetite had deserted him. In the end he drank a cup of coffee and ate a chocolate wafer he found in an otherwise empty tin. How could one relax and have a proper meal with two bloody policemen sitting waiting for you? He cursed: it wasn't fair, all the advantages lay with the other side. He was one against so many. He pulled himself abruptly together: he had never yet indulged in self-pity and this was no time to start.

As he stepped out on to the pavement, one of the officers leant back and opened the door for him. He got in, and, without anyone speaking, the car pulled away from the kerb.

The police station, which was a divisional headquarters, was a Victorian structure of dingy appearance on the main road about a mile and a half from Wise's home. On arrival he was led through a forbidding frosted-glass door, along a depressing passage and up a stone staircase, until they reached a door labelled "Detective-Superintendent". His guide knocked and then held the door open for Wise to enter.

"Come in and sit down, Mr. Wise. Get your meal all right?" Manton was sitting behind a cluttered desk, and indeed the whole room gave the impression of becoming slowly submerged under paper. He now picked up the telephone and said, "I'd like those reports, please."

Wise lent back in his chair and assumed an air of quiet expectancy. He had no idea what was going to happen, but a test of wits seemed certain, particularly as Manton was observing him as he might a squirrel in a cage.

There was a knock on the door and a uniformed constable entered. "You wanted these reports, sir," he said. But it was apparent to Wise that he was of far greater interest to the officer than any documents. For a full half-minute they stared at each other until Manton said firmly, "Thank you, Franklyn. Tell Detective-Sergeant Grant I'd like to see him."

The constable seemed to have difficulty in tearing his gaze away from Wise, but finally did so and left the room.

Manton gave Wise a solemn wink and began to hum, so that Wise wondered whether he was in a police station or participating in a children's television programme.

He heard footsteps approaching along the corridor, and mingled with them another sound which he couldn't at first identify. Then suddenly it came to him, and he felt as if a tongue of flame had seared his skin, for there too, unmistakably, was the tap-tap of a stick along the bare floor of the passage.

He glanced at Manton, who was continuing to watch him intently with alert bright blue eyes. Putting on a puzzled expression, he looked toward the door. Any second now it was going to open and admit Patrick Fox. He felt rivulets of sweat running down his back. His lips and mouth were parched. But this was a moment of truth and he must face it as he was. Nothing could now save him from meeting it: no "pax" was permissible.

The door was pushed and held open and Fox was guided into the room and to a chair directly opposite Wise's.

Manton spoke. "Mr. Fox, I'm going to ask you to listen to a voice and then tell me if you recognise it." He looked across at Wise. "Say something in your ordinary voice."

Wise ran his tongue over his lips and swallowed. This was it.

"Good evening, Mr. Fox, I don't know whether you remember me. I used to work for Mr. Gracey and have been to mend your radio once or twice."

He finished speaking and was aware that Manton was staring at him through half-closed eyes, rather with the air of a player who had believed he held all the trumps only to find himself pipped. Slowly he turned his head. "Do you recognise that voice, Mr. Fox?"

"Yes, I do, though I couldn't have placed it unless he'd reminded me."

"Do you know his name?"

"No, I don't think I've ever heard it."

Wise closed his eyes. He wanted to hurl himself across the room and hug the old man. What a friend!

"Are you sure he isn't the person you know as Peter Fox?"

"'Course he isn't Peter boy. I'd know *his* voice at once."

"But you've no idea what's happened to him?"

"I've told you I haven't, but I'm not worrying. Peter boy will turn up again one day all right. And if that's all, will you kindly take me home now?"

Manton nodded at Detective-Sergeant Grant, who led Fox from the room. "And you can go," he added to Wise. "I suppose you feel entitled to a free ride, too."

"You didn't seem to have any difficulty in arranging one to bring me here."

Manton smiled wryly. "You've got some cheek." He rose and walked over to the door. "We're engaged in a curious battle of wits, you and I, aren't we?" Observing Wise's buttoned-up expression, he added quickly, "It's all right, you're not expected to make any reply to that one."

Wise returned home in a thoroughly thoughtful frame of mind. His sense of reprieve was offset by the knowledge that Manton firmly believed him to be concerned in Goodwin's disappearance. Previously he had known he was under suspicion, but now it was something more than that. The failure to produce evidence against him had not only not diminished their suspicion, but had, in Manton's case, apparently raised it to certainty. This in turn meant that there would be no early end to the war of attrition to which he was being subjected.

He was glad to reach home, and experienced a greater than usual sense of relief and security as he locked the front door behind him. The peril of his position served to sharpen his appreciation of his home, and he saw with fresh eyes even those items which he had come to take for granted. They suddenly became faithful friends and allies, his chairs and carpets, his bed and his gay bathroom, his coloured walls and his drawings. He embraced them all now with a fond expression as he moved about the flat. Police inquires might have had the effect of placing him in quarantine, but they couldn't deprive him of the deep satisfaction he experienced just by being in his home.

It was the next evening that he suffered a further shock: this time another newspaper item.

"Police frogmen search canal," ran a head-line, and beneath it: "Police frogmen today searched part of the Western Trunk Canal in connection with the disappearance last Saturday of Mr. Geoffrey Goodwin, the author, of whom no trace has yet been found. Detective-Superintendent Manton and other officers were present while the search took place."

He turned quickly to the stop-press to learn the worst. "Canal search (see page 6)," he read. "A suitcase was recovered and taken to police headquarters for examination. Search meanwhile continues."

The next day the papers carried the additional imformation that a second suitcase had been fished out of the canal and that everything pointed to the two pieces of luggage as having belonged to Mr. Geoffrey Goodwin who had mysteriously disappeared. The evening papers of the same day informed their readers that the woods and fields in the area of Goodwin's cottage were being combed by police with tracker-dogs for possible clues to his whereabouts.

Since the nearest piece of Goodwin's body was buried a good four miles from where he had lived Wise wasn't unduly concerned. The recovery of the suitcases, so far as he could see, would serve merely to strengthen police suspicion of foul play, though in Manton's case it hadn't seemed that any strengthening was required. Wise was confident that there was nothing to link the disposal of the suitcases with himself. Nevertheless, he expected a further visitation from Manton, and duly received one that same evening. He was accompanied by Detective-Sergeant Grant.

It lasted an hour, during which time Manton pressingly questioned him all over again concerning Goodwin's visit to his flat. There were blunt questions and subtle questions, accusing questions and friendly questions, and questions of every other descriptive shade. Wise, however, remained calm and unshaken, and emerged from the stalemate the moral victor.

After Manton had gone, Wise made yet another check to ensure that he had overlooked nothing which might connect him with the crime. He was quite certain that he hadn't, but if you live in the hurricane belt you can never check too often that you're equipped to meet the onslaught. He went from room to room, cupboard to cupboard and drawer to drawer, but no, nothing remained. He had even, after Manton's first visit, destroyed the hat and the pair of spectacles which had formed his disguise as Peter Fox when he went to the United Bank to draw out the six thousand pounds.

Six thousand pounds! Well, people had been murdered for considerably less even though his own hopes had at one time been in terms of twenty times that amount.

A week, ten days went by without any fresh developments being reported in the Press and without further visits from the police. Lesley Gracey's phone calls had become more frequent, but he had managed to stave off her coming to see him.

All in all, he was learning to live quite equably with his lot, which was not unlike coming to terms with his own personal H-bomb, and was prepared to continue for as long as was necessary, when Manton appeared without warning on his doorstep one evening.

"I'm arresting you, Wise," he said, "on a charge of murdering Geoffrey Goodwin."

13

As Manton spoke, he stepped inside the door, followed by the silent Inspector Winslow and Detective-Sergeant Grant.

Wise was too stunned to speak or even to move. His brain fluttered feebly like a small pinioned bird. How could they arrest him? There'd been nothing in the newspapers to indicate they even contemplated such a move. Surely they hadn't discovered Goodwin's body and kept the matter secret. What had been happening without his knowledge? Arrest him? It was unthinkable. As though from a great distance, he heard Manton saying something about not being obliged to make any reply in answer to the charge. That was it, he was being cautioned. In these days the words of the caution were as well known as the opening lines of the National Anthem.

"Are you ready, Wise, or do you want to get some other clothes? You won't be seeing your flat again for some time."

These last words had the effect of an electric current passing through him. His brain cleared and he wanted to cry out in agony—an agony occasioned by the sudden realisation that he was about to be wrenched from his home. His eyes pricked with tears.

"I'd put on a jacket of some sort, if I were you," Manton went on. "That and the clothes you're wearing are all you'll want."

They followed him upstairs and into the bedroom. Sergeant Grant then accompanied him as he went round on the last-minute errands before departure. Gas, electricity and water were turned off, windows were secured and things were put away out of sight, though this was preceded by another search of all his property.

"Got a hat?" Manton asked, apparently casually.

Wise shook his head. "I never wear one."

"Sit on the sofa a few minutes. I'd like to take a look at your desk."

Wise sat down. There was no point in protesting, for his brain told him that he must concentrate his energies where they could do some good and not squander them on futile gestures. He watched Manton go carefully through the contents of his desk, knowing he'd find nothing incriminating.

"Is this your only bank account?" Manton asked, holding up a statement.

"Yes." It related to Colin Wise's account with the local branch of the London and Counties Bank and showed a credit balance of £48 16s. 5d.

Manton slipped the account, together with some cheque stubs, into his pocket and continued his search. He must have spent half an hour checking every piece of paper he could lay his hands on before he was ready to go.

Wise braced himself. This was the moment he had most been dreading, that of physical departure. As they stepped outside, Manton said, "Lock the door and give me the key. We'll probably need to come back." He noticed Wise's hesitation. "You don't have to worry, you can always sue us if you find anything missing. Suing the police is quite a pastime these days, isn't it, Inspector?" Inspector Winslow nodded solemnly, and Manton added, "Always of course in your case if you get the opportunity of returning."

Wise clenched his jaws to hide the bubbling of emotion he felt within him. In one quick movement he locked the door, handed the key to Manton and resolutely turned his back on his home.

When they were in the car, Manton remarked conversationally, "Most arrested men ask many more questions than you have. In fact you haven't asked any. Isn't there anything you'd like to know? I should have thought there was one matter you'd be particularly curious about."

Wise saw Sergeant Grant grin. Well, let him grin, he wasn't going to give them the satisfaction of asking questions. He'd say nothing, just behave quietly and let them speculate. He'd done his fair share of the latter during the past two weeks, now it was their turn. It would take more than arrest and police bonhomie to break him down, as they were on the verge of discovering.

When they arrived at the police station, Wise was formally charged and cautioned by a uniformed inspector in Manton's presence and he gave a peremptory shake of his head when invited to make a reply.

It was getting on for eleven o'clock when he was given an armful of blankets and locked into one of the cells. He didn't even give them the satisfaction of asking what came next. He curled up in the blankets but remained tensely wakeful. He heard a distant church clock strike midnight, one, two, three and four o'clock before sleep finally claimed him for two brief hours.

He was aching and stiff when he awoke, and his skin itched, as it always did after sleeping in his clothes. An elderly constable arrived with a razor, a shaving brush and a stick of soap that was the colour of old candle.

"You'll have to make do with this lot," he said, leading Wise to a washbasin at the end of the row of cells. Wise grimaced. The idea of using a communal shaving brush filled him with distaste, but there was no alternative, and, anyway, he did feel better afterwards.

Back in his cell, the same officer brought him a bowl of porridge, a mug of tea and a tin plate on which rested two greasy rashers of bacon and two doorsteps of bread thinly spread with margarine.

"Here's your breakfast," he said affably. "Mayn't look up to much but you'd better eat it. No knowing when you'll get another chance."

Wise rejected the porridge and made a bacon sandwich. As he ate this without much appetite, he tortured himself with the thought that his own home lay less than two miles away. Then he stopped himself. He mustn't surrender to morbid thinking, he mustn't drift fatalistically. He must start to fight back, to extricate himself. Soon he would know what the police had been able to muster against him and would be able to make his own plans accordingly.

Just after nine o'clock Manton appeared in his cell door. "How are you feeling this morning?"

"All right."

"You'll be appearing in court shortly. It'll only be formal, and I shall be asking for a remand in custody, which means you'll go to Brixton Prison." Wise made no reply, and Manton went on, "Before you go to court, you're being put up on an identification parade. That'll be in about a quarter of an hour's time. No objections, I take it. Good!"

Leaving Colin Wise to ponder this, he went off. Wise lay back on his bed and chewed his lower lip as he tried to think for what reason the parade was to be held. Who on earth had caught the sort of glimpse of him that could require the confirmation or otherwise of a formal identification parade?

He was still anxiously pondering when he was fetched by a constable and led through to a yard at the back of the station, where about a dozen men stood in sheepish groups. He had just taken in the fact that they were all bespectacled and all wearing hats, when one of the officers present handed him the same two items.

"Put those on."

A uniformed inspector—the same one who had charged him the previous evening—lined the men up and then explained to Wise that he could take up any position he wished. Wise selected a place three from the right-hand end and noted that the men either side of him shot sidelong glances of intense interest.

"Now if you'd all look straight to your front I'll have the witness fetched," said the inspector.

From the same door through which Wise had emerged there now came the clerk from the Shepherd's Bush branch of the United Bank who had cashed the cheque and handed him the six thousand pounds. Wise had guessed it would be him as soon as he'd been told to put on the hat and spectacles. Luckily the hat was quite different both in colour and shape from the one he'd been wearing, which seemed to indicate that the clerk was uncertain about this particular feature.

He walked down the line like an extremely nervous inspecting notable. When he reached the end, he gave the uniformed inspector a helpless shrug. They whispered together for a second before the inspector called out, "Will you now all take your hats off, please?"

The clerk returned along the line, but it was apparent to Wise from his expression that he was in no danger of recognition.

The parade broke up and Manton came over to him. "You won't go on having so much luck, Wise."

Colin Wise gave him a mild look. He felt inclined to remark acidly on his abrupt translation from "Mr. Wise" before arrest to "Wise" after, but ruled this out as belonging to the class of "futile gesture" he had made up his mind to resist.

"I hardly called being arrested having luck," he said instead.

"It depends what happens afterwards!" Manton smiled wryly. "But if you ask me, you've had a fair whack of luck. Perhaps you deserve it. You'll certainly need it."

Obsessed with his own thoughts these past twelve hours, it had not occurred to Wise that he had overnight become a figure of enormous public interest. Accordingly, he was amazed to observe the phalanx of photographers who were grouped round the exit of the police station yard, and his escort shielded his face from a dozen cameras as the car taking him to court swung out into the road.

On arrival at court he was placed in another cell and left to his own devices. It had already been brought home to him that he was going to be provided with plenty of time to think in the coming days. Being someone who was quite happy in his own company, he viewed this prospect with less dismay than would most and prayed that he wouldn't have to share a cell at any stage of his incarceration. The very prospect filled him with disgust.

After an hour he was fetched by a red-faced sergeant, and a minute or so later found himself in court and the centre of interest of a hundred pairs of eyes.

It was the first time he had ever been inside a court, though a quick glance about him as he was shown into the dock confirmed a scene he had viewed often enough on television. The raised dais on which the magistrates had their seats, the clerk just below them, the dock which he found himself sharing with a constable of mournful expression, and tiers of eager faces on all sides. He was aware that even the lawyers in the rows just in front of him were constantly turning their heads to give him appraising glances. The Press over to his left watched him, with pencils sharpened and imaginations as sensitive as photographic plates.

It flashed across Wise's mind that he and his mournful escort ought to do something more than just stand there and stare back to justify all the attention.

"Is your name Colin Wise?" the clerk of the court now asked. Wise nodded. "You are charged with the murder of Geoffrey Goodwin at a place unknown on or about the 20th March. Do you understand the charge?" Wise nodded again. The clerk looked toward Manton, who had taken up position in the witness-box. "I understand, Superintendent, that you are asking for a week's remand in custody?"

"I am, your worship."

"Very well, will you give short evidence of arrest?"

Wise pricked his ears. He had better listen carefully to this, but though he did so he heard nothing which he could dispute. As Manton was finishing, Wise's attention turned to the three magistrates sitting on the bench, who rather looked as though they had wandered in off the street for a short rest before continuing on their daily round. The presiding one was a woman: she wore a brown felt hat, and a bulging handbag was perched on the desk in front of her. It didn't require much imagination to see a shopping basket near her feet. She was flanked by two men of nondescript appearance.

Wise suddenly became aware that the female magistrate was addressing him.

"Do you wish to ask the superintendent any questions?" He shook his head. "Then we remand you in custody until this day week."

There was a whispered colloquy between her and the clerk, to which the two other magistrates bent their heads, then the clerk turned round and asked, "Do you want legal aid?"

Wise had been warned that this would come and had, not without reluctance, decided to accept the offer. His first inclination had been to defend himself and not rely on someone about whom he knew nothing to fight the most important battle of his life, but he had realised that, having become entangled with the law, it would be more prudent to have recourse to the services of one of its own minions. It was his very last intention, however, to sit passively back and give some unknown quantity a free hand with his future life.

"Yes, please," he said quietly in answer to the clerk's question.

"We grant that application," the lady magistrate replied indulgently, although Wise had been under the impression that it was *they* who had been offering him something. But, of course, this was the law, the land of spiralling jargon and of chessboard formulae.

Soon after he had been returned to his cell, the redfaced sergeant appeared.

"Who'd you want to defend you?"

"Who can I have?"

"If you take my advice you'll have Mr. Figgis. He's very popular in this court is Mr. Figgis. You won't go far wrong with him."

"Who else is there?"

"No one as good as Mr. Figgis."

"Do you get a cut out of this? Is that why you're so keen on my having Mr. Figgis?"

The sergeant glared. "You'll get a cut if you're not careful. Now is it to be Mr. Figgis?"

"No. At least not until I know more about him and about the others I could have. Isn't there a list?"

The sergeant slammed the cell door and retired. Some time went by and then a young man appeared.

"Mr. Grayson, the clerk, sent me," he announced cheerfully. "I understand you want to see the names of the solicitors on the Legal Aid list." He handed Wise a piece of paper. "You can take your pick."

"Who would you have if you were me?" Wise asked, taking a chance, but he rather liked the look of the clerk's assistant, who could be no older than himself. "I'd like somebody young," he added.

"Mr. Colbourne's young: gives you pretty good value for money, too. Not, of course, that it's your money." He grinned.

"The ratepayers fork out to prosecute you while the taxpayers foot the bill for your defence. The March Hare couldn't have devised it better. Mr. Colbourne, then?"

"Is he better than Mr. Figgis?"

"From your point of view, yes. Mr. Figgis is all right, but he belongs to the establishment, if you know what I mean. Incidentally, I shouldn't be surprised if one or two newspapers don't try and get in touch with you about financing your defence."

"What would they expect to get in return?"

"Oh, just the choicest pickings of your life to date."

Wise frowned. "Well, you can tell them from me they're wasting their time. I'll take Mr. Colbourne."

"Fine, and I'll give the Press your message."

"When do I see my solicitor?"

"He'll certainly be here at the remand hearing next week, but he'll probably come and visit you in Brixton before then."

As the young man turned to go, Wise said gratefully, "Thanks for your help."

"That's O.K., glad to have been of service," he replied cheerfully. "By the way, any objection to giving me your autograph?" He produced a small autograph book out of his pocket. "It's for my kid brother." Wise gave him a wary look. "I promise you there's no catch," he added, disarmingly.

Wise signed his name on a blank page. "It's not worth much, I'm afraid," he remarked. "Not yet, maybe," the young man agreed with unmistakable meaning.

Like the Cheshire cat, his grin lingered after the rest of him had departed, leaving Wise once more alone to ponder his fate. It was late afternoon before he was fetched from his cell by the red-faced sergeant. "Come on, your car's waiting."

In the yard behind the courthouse was parked a mobile cell van of solid appearance, of a type which Wise had frequently seen before but only from the outside. A number of the cells were already occupied, and he received a noisy welcome as he was locked into one and the van set off on its journey to Brixton Prison. He soon made it clear, however, that he wasn't in any mood to join in the bawdily facetious repartee that shuttled between the passengers. The journey seemed endless, as several halts were made to pick up additional prisoners, and the inability to see out added to its discomfort.

His first view of the inside of the prison was less forbidding than he had expected. As he and the others stepped out, the herding and shouting began. To his dismay, he found himself almost immediately locked into another cell—this time one in the reception block, to await the pleasure of medical and prison officers who supervised the depressing process known as reception.

As he sat in this cell he knew that it had been the worst day of his life. Almost every hour had brought a fresh test of nerves, a further confrontation with the unknown, though this had only served to make him seek refuge within himself and to shun the atmosphere of specious confidences in which he found himself projected.

He heard cell doors being unlocked, and a second later his own was thrown open.

"Come on, you lot, out," shouted an officer with a much pleasanter face than Wise had ever expected to see in prison service uniform.

For the next half-hour they were herded in and out of rooms and along corridors, being documented, medically examined, showered and finally issued with a few basic essentials. Wise found that he could continue wearing his own clothes if he wished, and elected to do so.

As they emerged from the reception block not far from where they'd entered it, a fresh batch of prisoners was being fed on to the conveyer belt, and so, as he was shortly to see, it continued almost round the clock.

"Behave yourself and you'll be O.K.," he had heard an officer say to one of his fellow-prisoners, which was another way of saying, "Lose your personality, be unobtrusive, melt into the grey background." Well, he was prepared to do this, to play along with authority. If the officers wanted to be called "Sir" he'd call them "Sir", however much he might secretly despise them.

He was taken across to the hospital block and put in the charge of a white-coated hospital officer.

"You're the bloke what's murdered that writer chap, aren't you?" he asked in a conversational tone as he led Wise up a caged-in staircase.

"That's what I'm charged with."

"I get your point."

He unlocked a barred door, locking it again behind them, and pushed his way through a pair of ordinary swing doors into a large, airy ward with about twenty beds.

"That's your bed over there." He went up to another officer who was sitting playing draughts at a large table in the centre of the room. "This is 5386 Wise, murder remand."

Wise went slowly across to his bed. It was narrow and covered by a green spread. He put a hand on it and pressed. It was as springy as the road outside. Over the rail at the head was a pair of earphones. That was something he hadn't expected to find in prison. A glance showed him that every bed was similarly equipped, and indeed several men were lying on their beds listening to the radio.

"Did I hear him say your name was Wise?"

Wise turned and found that it was the occupant of the next bed who had spoken. He was a small, shrivelled man with a bald head and a childishly eager expression. He was sitting on the edge of his bed, swinging his legs and watching Wise with hopeful interest. In another setting he would have worn the hallmarks of the club bore.

"Yes."

"I've just been reading all about you in the evening paper. We get papers here, you know; we're still the élite, we're only on remand, but it's different once you've been convicted. There's quite a long piece, would you like to see it?"

"Thanks."

"I'll show it to you in a minute. You don't mind my chatting to you, do you?"

"No."

"Some of them only want to read or listen to the radio all day, but I like a bit of conversation. By the way, my name's Pooler, Edwin Pooler." He beamed proudly. "Though I'm better know as Inky Pooler."

"Why's that?" Wise asked dutifully.

"Because I once fell into a vat of ink trying to get away after one of my jobs." He laughed uproariously in recollection of this entertaining episode, and Wise found himself smiling too. There was something engaging about his eagerness to be companionable.

"What type of job was that one?"

"I'm what's known as an arsonist," he said with quiet dignity.

"Weren't you afraid of getting burnt by your own fire?"

"No, that one went out before the fire brigade arrived," he replied in a primly regretful tone. His expression cleared and he looked at Colin Wise with something near to hero worship. "I'd never have the nerve to murder anyone, and to think they can't even find the body."

"I haven't murdered anyone either," Wise said firmly.

"That's all right, you needn't be afraid of me, I shan't grass."

"I tell you I didn't murder Goodwin."

But Pooler wasn't listening. "Of course you realise yours will be a D.P.P. case?"

"What's that?"

"Director of Public Prosecutions. He only does the big cases. You can always tell—his briefs have white tape, the others have pink." He looked suddenly crestfallen. "Only one of my cases has ever been done by the D.P.P.," he said unhappily. "You'd think arson was important enough for him, wouldn't you?"

Wise shook his head. "I've no idea."

"I'd hoped he'd be in my present case, but he's not. And after I'd set fire to a baptist chapel, too." He became thoughtful. "Perhaps it's because it was a disused one and very little damage was done. I think it must have been damp." He gave a resigned sigh. "But I'm sure I still have a good chance of coming up before the red judge. I'm an Old Bailey case, of course."

"Oh?"

"Yes, Quarter Sessions can't deal with arson," he said severely.

"I didn't know."

"You'll be before the red judge, too. Murder always is."

"What is this red judge?" Wise asked.

"The High Court Judge who goes down to the Old Bailey each session to preside over the most important cases. They have a whole lot of lesser judges who sit permanently for the smaller crimes. I once came up in one of their courts because they'd reduced the original charge against me. It was very drab and colourless. And none of the connoisseurs you always find in the public gallery of Number One Court."

"You must have spent a great deal of time inside."

"I have. And do you know what?" He leaned forward to whisper conspiratorially, "They're going to try and prove I'm insane this time. It's disgraceful, isn't it?" Wise made a sympathetic face. "Of course you know they'll be making a full medical report on you?"

"They?"

"The doctors here. What's more, they have you kept under constant observation up here in the ward. That chap over there playing draughts will keep a record of how many times you turn over in the night, whether you belch with your breakfast or your dinner, how often you take a piddle. Oh yes, boy, they'll be watching you all right. After all, you're a celebrity with what you've done."

Wise glanced round the ward and at its occupants engaged in various desultory pursuits. He couldn't see one of whom he would care to make a friend, even if he'd wanted to, which he didn't. They were a shifty, seedy-looking bunch of have-nots with whom he could feel no kinship whatsoever. Prison had always been their inevitable fate, whereas for him it was a ditch into which he had skidded and would soon be out of without too much damage.

He felt Inky Pooler tugging at his sleeve. "I think you and me'll get on. I can always tell. Some of these others are just slobs. That fellow on the opposite bed, for example, killed his baby daughter. Blokes like him shouldn't be allowed to have children. He's crazy, of course. The one next to him murdered his mother-in-law: says he wishes he'd done it before. And next to him is a bloke who tried to murder his wife's lover: reckon they've got the wrong one inside there. And the one playing draughts, he keeps on committing bigamy and they reckon he's a nut case. You married, by the way?"

"No."

"I was once. Don't know what happened to her. She was there when I went to prison and gone when I came out. Never seen or heard of her since."

"What time do we have to go to bed?" Wise asked, feeling that he'd had sufficient of Inky Pooler's company for the time being.

"Lights out at nine. We get cocoa first. Up at half-past six. It's a long day unless you've got someone to talk to, but you and me'll be all right."

Wise noticed that several occupants had undressed, and he decided to do likewise. He moved round to the other side of his bed and turned his back on Pooler, who was smiling contentedly at no one in particular and swinging his legs. A young man with a pale, pointed face, who was lying on the next bed, looked up from the magazine he was reading and said tensely, "This place is worse than the bloody army and I didn't think anything could be. And I've got a wife and a baby to worry about, too. I heard you say you weren't married. Well, you're lucky, mate, if you're going to spend the next few years inside."

"I'm not," Wise snapped, and turned away. He began to undress and then lay down on top of his bed with his hands laced beneath his head. He didn't join the queue for cocoa when it arrived, and slipped beneath the blankets shortly before lights out.

Although he had not slept more than a couple of hours the previous night, and the day had taken its toll of his nervous energy, he had never felt more wide awake. It was almost as if he had swallowed a handful of pep pills. Last night had been bad enough, but at least he had been in a cell by himself. Now he felt like a crab which has had its shell suddenly ripped away. He was lonely, though without wanting company, and was deeply miserable. It was going to require all his mental resources to maintain the calm façade of innocence he had determined upon. It would be easier once things began moving, once he knew what he had to meet, but he realised he might have to wait two or three weeks before the prosecution was ready to proceed with their case in the magistrates' court, and until then it could only be a long enervating drain.

The night officer paused at the end of his bed and regarded him. "Want a sleeping pill?"

"No thanks." He'd either sleep without aid or he wouldn't sleep. The officer passed on and resumed his seat at a small table over by the door.

Wise continued his blank study of the darkened ceiling. Forget the present, he told himself, think of the future. Think what you'll do with that six thousand pounds. Think of the new life you'll be able to make for yourself. In his mind's eye he saw himself driving up in a smart red sports coupé to a secluded but not large villa set on a sunny hillside with a wide view over blue sea. It would be furnished with perfect taste, nothing garish or ostentatious, but everything unmistakably right. On the walls would be the pictures of a small but selective purchaser. The image dimmed as almost against his will sleep finally overtook him.

The next morning beds had been made, breakfast eaten and Colin Wise, who was temporarily relieved of Inky Pooler's persistent presence, had an opportunity of examining his surroundings in the light of a new day.

Apart from Pooler, no one had attempted to cultivate his company, and it was apparent that most of the ward's occupants chose to maintain attitudes of reserve in relation to one another. Camaraderie might be forced upon them or even come as a welcome outlet after conviction, when they were cast on to the heaving human slag heap which is the nation's prison population. But for the moment they were prisoners on remand who still had hope of wriggling off the hook and of returning to the dark corners of their previous lives.

But with hope there also went uncertainty—uncertainty which was reflected in their withdrawn expressions and in the furtive looks they flicked about them and which would be removed only by a jury's verdict. Until then they would be alternately torn by hope and despair, and be consumed by a listlessness which would be as paralysing as any drug-produced reaction. Wise felt confident that with his superior intelligence he would be better able than the others to combat the insidious drain of prison existence on his resources.

Inky Pooler returned to the ward just before morning exercise and fastened himself on to Wise as they were taken downstairs, and under the watchful eyes of two officers put in motion round a small oval circuit outside the hospital block. Colin Wise had planned to shake him off simply by walking faster than he could, but such hopes were frustrated by the shambling pace set by those in front. He noticed a number of faces other than those from his own ward, and asked Pooler who they were.

"They're from other wards," his companion replied with a sniff. "All the important cases are in ours, of course. These are mostly Sessions cases. Minor sex offences, feeble-minded burglars and the like." His tone indicated clearly his disdain for those who didn't aspire to be dealt with by red judges at Assizes or prosecuted by the Director of Public Prosecutions.

Half-way through the period of exercise Wise heard his name called out and went across to an officer who had just come out of the hospital block.

"Wise?"

"Yes, sir."

"Dr. Fleming wants to see you. In case you don't know, he's the principal medical officer here."

Dr. Fleming, rotund, rosy-cheeked and with a shock of iron-grey hair, sat white-coated behind a desk.

"Sit in that chair, Wise," he said, indicating one the other side of the desk. He nodded at the hospital officer. "O.K., Bell."

As soon as he had spoken, Wise had recognised a West Country accent and been suddenly reminded of Uncle Tom and the farm at Farthingmoor. Dr. Fleming, for his part, gave the new arrival a sharply appraising study. He didn't look the sort to murder and mysteriously dispose of his victim's body, but thirty years in the prison medical service had taught him that no one, least of all those charged with murder, could be judged by appearances. Accordingly, even though Wise had no record of violence, he quietly slid open the drawer containing the two feet of solid ebony ruler which had saved his life on one occasion.

"First of all, some questions about your family and background," he said, picking up a pen and opening the buff folder in front of him. "Are your parents alive?"

"I've never known my parents."

Dr. Fleming evinced no surprise at this disclosure as Wise went on to tell him as much he was able of his antecedents.

"Ever suffered any serious illnesses?"

"None."

"And you've never been in any sort of trouble before?"

"No."

"Anything you'd like to tell me about the offence with which you're now charged?"

"I never murdered Mr. Goodwin. I've no idea what's happened to him. All I know is that I've been unjustly accused."

Dr. Fleming's expression revealed nothing as he wrote hard for a minute or two. He looked up and said, "You don't seem unduly depressed at your present position?"

"Well, I'm not happy about it, I can tell you that, sir, but I'm confident I'll get off."

"Because you're innocent?"

"I *am* innocent."

"Now a few questions about your sex life. Quite normal, is it?"

"I think so."

There followed a series of probing questions at the end of which the doctor remarked drily, "You seem to be unusually well adjusted in that direction, I congratulate you." He nodded towards an examination couch in a corner of the room. "Get up on that, would you? I'll just check your heart and blood pressure." When this was done, he said, "That's all for now. I'll be seeing you quite often, however, in the coming few weeks. As you probably know, I'm required to make a full report on you for the court of trial. Your solicitors will automatically receive a copy, too. Incidentally, I shall be getting in touch with Mr. and Mrs. Pritchard." He paused, with one eyebrow slightly raised.

"That doesn't mean that I have to see them, does it?"

"Not if you don't wish to."

"I don't."

"All right, Wise."

A second later Hospital Officer Bell appeared, and Wise was

111

taken back upstairs to the ward. Exercise was finished and Inky Pooler pounced on him as soon as he entered.

"How did it go? Was it Dr. Fleming?"

"Yes."

"He always sees all the murder cases personally," he said in a glow of reflected glory. "He'll be present throughout your trial, too." He smiled wistfully. "You really get top treatment all round when you're a murder case."

"If you're so envious why don't you commit one yourself?" Wise asked tartly.

Inky Pooler sighed. "Murderers are born, not made."

Wise turned away impatiently. He was tired of being placed on such a dubious pedestal, and wished his cloying companion had managed to get caught in one of his own fires.

Newspapers had arrived and he went over to the centre table to look at one. There was a full account of his brief appearance in court the previous day, with the additional ominous piece of information that police inquiries were being stepped up. This was followed by a short paragraph from the paper's legal correspondent, who reported that, contrary to popular belief, a murder charge could be preferred even though the victim's body was never found. He cited two cases in the past fifteen years where convictions had been obtained in such circumstances, though admitting that the absence of a body made things more difficult for the prosecution as they had to rely on circumstantial evidence to prove that a death had taken place and that murder was the only possible inference. This was an easier matter, he pointed out, where the murder was alleged to have been committed on the high seas as it had been in one of the two cases he referred to.

Wise pushed the newspaper away from him. How could anyone, even the Director of Public Prosecutions and all the red judges put together, prove that Goodwin was dead unless they found his body, and that, he was confident, they would never do. He hoped that Mr. Colbourne, his solicitor, would visit him soon in prison, as he felt more than ever the need, not so much to talk as to ask questions. For days he had been bottling up questions which filled his mind and which, provided Mr.

Colbourne gained his confidence, would come pouring forth for answer.

His hope was fulfilled sooner than he'd dared expect, for that afternoon, just before exercise, he was fetched from the ward and taken across to the interview block, which lay across the way from the hospital. It was a one-storey building with ten or so rooms off a long corridor, half-way down which sat a chief officer.

"Room four," he said, as Wise and his escort came up.

Mr. Colbourne was already in the room and stepped forward with his hand outstretched as Wise entered.

"Hello, Wise, I'm Colbourne." His manner was brisk and he had an alert expression. He was short, wore spectacles and had plastered-down, brown wavy hair. Wise reckoned he wasn't yet thirty.

They sat down at the table and the solicitor produced a notebook from his briefcase. "You don't need to worry," he said in a matter-of-fact tone, "this is the one place in the prison where you can talk freely."

Wise glanced around the small, depressing room. A pair of bedraggled chintz curtains and a chocolate-box picture on the wall of three oddly coloured dogs lying in front of a log fire were the only adornments. There was an inner window, and Wise found it difficult not to look up every time somebody passed along the corridor.

"I didn't really expect you to come so soon," he said. "But I'm very glad you have."

"I always like to see clients at the earliest possible moment." He flattened the page of his notebook. "Now then, I understand our defence will be that you didn't murder Goodwin?" Wise nodded. "Nevertheless, you *were* the last person to see him."

"So they say."

"And can probably prove."

"But how do they know he's dead?"

Mr. Colbourne looked sharply inquiring. "You'd better tell me everything you've told the police to date, as well as everything you think they might have against you."

When Wise had finished, Mr. Colbourne sat back and frowned at the notes he had been taking.

"And that's the lot?"

"Yes."

"You're quite sure there's nothing else they can turn up which you haven't told me about?"

"No, I can't think of anything," Wise replied slowly.

"Because," Mr. Colbourne went on meaningly, "there's nothing worse for a solicitor or counsel than being taken by surprise by something which their client hasn't mentioned. Nothing worse for the client, that is."

"I understand," Wise said, meeting his solicitor's steady gaze, "but I've told you everything."

Mr. Colbourne appeared thoughtful. "Then they must have something more we don't know about. They couldn't charge you simply on what you've told me."

Wise felt a prickle of fear run along his spine, for the solicitor was only confirming his own anxiety. But what? What would the police have found out?

The solicitor gave a shrug. "We shall just have to wait until we hear their case."

"Isn't there a chance of finding out something before then?" Wise asked in a worried tone.

"I'll keep my ears open, of course, but they're being pretty cagey and I mayn't be able to pick up much. Those they've interviewed have obviously been told not to let anything leak out."

"When will the prosecution or whatever it's called start?"

"They certainly won't be ready by the next remand date. Possibly the one after that, but we won't let them get away with indefinite postponement, don't worry."

"I still don't see what evidence they can have got against me."

"I'm pretty sure they wouldn't have charged you without first consulting the Director of Public Prosecutions, so they must have something. That's why I said it was very important you should tell me everything they may have been able to dig up."

"Supposing Mr. Goodwin's still alive?"

"The absence of a victim's body is obviously the weakest link in their case," Mr. Colbourne remarked.

"And what about the absence of any motive I had for killing Mr. Goodwin?" He shook his head in despair. "I'm certain you'll find that he's disappeared like this before. Just gone off into the blue."

"Don't worry, that'll be one of dozens of inquiries I'll be making. Though frankly I don't see why he should first have thrown all his luggage into the canal."

Nor did Wise, but he said, "All part of the plan to hide the fact that he was intending to do a mysterious bunk."

"Still doesn't make sense," Mr. Colbourne retorted. "Anyway, if the prosecution is sufficiently thin we may be able to get the charge thrown out by the magistrates."

Wise assumed a hopeful expression and the solicitor added quickly, "But don't bank on that; the odds are you'll be sent for trial at the Old Bailey. Now is there anything else you want to ask me before our next meeting, which'll probably be at court when you come up on remand."

"Would a witness be helpful?"

"That's a rather odd way of putting it," Mr. Colbourne replied suspiciously. "A witness as to what?"

"There's somebody who could probably give evidence for me, but I'd sooner the person wasn't dragged in unless it's absolutely necessary."

Colin Wise could tell from his solicitor's expression that he had made an error in mentioning the matter in that particular way. He had made it sound as though he could buy the evidence, which was, of course, exactly what he could do, except that it wouldn't cost him anything. It was already paid for.

"We can discuss ` later," Mr. Colbourne said dismissively, "when we're in a better position to know whether your witness's testimony could really assist your defence." He rose and held out his hand. "Leave everything to me, Wise. You've got a darned sight better chance than most of the unfortunates in this establishment. At least you haven't opened your mouth to the police. I reckon we'll be able to put up a tough fight on this one." He nodded his head in a satisfied way. "This'll give you something to do. I'd like you to write out in statement form everything you've told me and anything else that occurs to you. You can also make a list of the points which you think to be in your favour. Will you do that?"

"I'll be glad to."

"Fine. See you at court next week, then."

When Colin Wise returned to the ward, he was feeling happier and more confident than at any time since his arrest. Mr. Colbourne's visit had proved a tonic, and he was delighted with the young clerk from the court office who had recommended him.

"Letter for you," the hospital officer on duty said, as he passed by his desk.

Though Colin Wise didn't know the writing on the envelope, he felt he could guess who it was from and opened it without enthusiasm.

"Darling Colin," he read, "I couldn't come to court this morning as there would have been a terrific row when Miss Duncan told Daddy that I had missed a class. I cried when I heard the awful news, but bear up, darling. I know everything will come right. It must. Please let me know how I can help you. There must be some way. I could come and see you if it was a Saturday or Sunday. Is there anything you need? Mummy and Daddy were talking about you when I came in this evening, but they changed the subject as soon as I opened the door. The police have been to see Daddy several times, but he won't talk about it. He thinks I'm now doing my French homework. He'd blow up if he knew I was writing to you. I long to get a letter from you, but Daddy would find out. But I promise I'll go on writing to you. Must close now. Good night, darling, and try and keep cheerful. God bless. Fondest love from Lesley."

Wise folded the letter with a thoughtful expression and slipped it into his pocket. It was early yet to decide whether to accept Lesley's offer of help, but since it would obviously remain open he could afford to let the idea simmer awhile. It would ultimately depend on what use he could make of her, and that he wouldn't be able to assess until he knew the details of the case against him. Meanwhile, he was at least absolved from replying to the letter, which was a matter for relief. He hoped she wouldn't try and come to court, though he thought he could probably rely on her father to frustrate any endeavours in that direction. He wondered why the police had been to see the old bastard several times. Presumably routine digging into his (Wise's) immediate past.

He walked across the ward and gazed out of one of the barred windows, still deep in thought. As he did so there slowly crystallised in his mind what was the most detestable feature of prison life. It was being under escort every time you moved. Even a dog on a lead had greater freedom than the small groups he was watching in shuffling progress from one building to another. You were fetched and taken and delivered and fetched again. You waited while a door was unlocked to let you pass: then you waited while it was re-locked before moving on to the next.

During the first few days he was not unduly bothered by the claustrophobic element of prison routine, but then he began to feel it so acutely that he looked forward to his forthcoming court appearance with all the eager impatience of a child waiting for the Christmas holidays. Saturdays and Sundays were particularly grim days, if only because of their reminder of how differently they were being spent by those outside. The circumstance of incarceration was really rubbed in over the weekend.

On the day of the remand hearing Wise was delivered to court shortly after half-past nine. The fat, red-faced sergeant greeted him with grumbling resignation.

"You back again? Time fair spins past, doesn't it?"

"For some perhaps," Wise observed sourly, as the cell door was firmly banged on him.

It opened next to reveal Mr. Colbourne, and Wise sprang hopefully to his feet.

"Thought I'd just let you know I'm here," the solicitor said. "We'll have a talk afterwards."

Even allowing for his normal briskness, there had been something disturbing about his manner—as though he was bracing himself to perform a disagreeable duty. But before Wise had time to ponder over it he was taken into court.

He purposely didn't gaze around him, as he had no wish to acknowledge the hesitant smiles and solemn nods of anyone he might recognise. Instead he focused his attention on Mr.

Colbourne, who rose to his feet as soon as Manton had made his formal application for a further seven days' remand in custody.

"I should like to ask Mr. Manton," he said in a wintry voice, "whether the prosecution will be ready to open their case next week?"

"As Mr. Colbourne is aware, the matter is now in the hands of the Director of Public Prosecutions."

"I am indeed aware of it, but I am sure Mr. Manton is sufficiently in the Director's confidence to be able to answer my question."

Manton, who was used to this kind of pressure from the defence—he could scarcely remember a case in which police inquiries hadn't been conducted against the calendar—looked appealingly toward the magistrates. If he could secure a further formal remand, it would mean that much more breathing-space both for himself and for Mr. Hunt, the D.P.P.'s man who would be representing the prosecution and who, incidentally, had already begun to spur him from the other flank. There were still large numbers of inquiries to be made, and he knew that if there was one thing the D.P.P.'s representatives disliked it was opening a case before the picture was complete. He didn't blame them, but it wasn't his fault. As usual it was the laboratory people who were holding up everything, though they in their turn would blame someone else. In the end it was invariably the officer in charge who collected the kicks.

"After all," Mr. Colbourne went on, in a suddenly sweet tone, "the police had apparently amassed sufficient evidence to arrest my client, so why aren't they ready to go ahead now if required?"

The lady chairman of the magistrates held a worried consultation with her colleagues and the clerk while Wise watched them from his stockade in the middle of the courtroom. It reminded him of an under-rehearsed play performed by amateurs who missed their cues, fluffed their lines and didn't know the first thing about acting. Perhaps it required Inky Pooler's red judge to inject the missing touch of drama into the proceedings.

The chairman now nervously addressed herself to Superintendent Manton. "We would like you to convey our hope that the case can be opened next week."

Manton bowed and threw Mr. Colbourne a stony look, and a few seconds later Wise was shepherded back to his cell. When his solicitor joined him, he said with heartfelt relief, "Thank God we're really going to get started next week."

Mr. Colbourne shot him a sharply appraising glance, then said abruptly, "Can you think of any reason, Wise, why the police should have gone to the trouble of removing the bath from your flat?"

14

There was no need for Colin Wise to simulate shock and outrage, for he experienced both in response to Mr. Colbourne's question. He felt like a householder who returns to find that his home has been ransacked in his absence, with the addition that his sense of shock was tinged by genuine alarm.

Mr. Colbourne, who had asked the question in the particular way in order to get a spontaneous reaction, said, "The inference is fairly obvious, I suppose."

"You mean, they believe I killed Mr. Goodwin in the bath? But that's absolutely crazy."

"Not necessarily that you *killed* him in the bath, but that you did something with the body there."

Wise shook his head as though he found it difficult to understand such outrageously wild insinuations. Then, frowning, he said, "It must be those scratch marks. . . ."

"What scratch marks" Mr. Colbourne asked sharply.

"There are three or four marks on the side and bottom of the bath." He looked his solicitor full in the face. "They've been there ages."

"What matters is how they got there."

Wise's brain worked overtime. He realised that his explanation must not only convince Mr. Colbourne but others, too, for he was likely to be stuck with it to the end.

"It happened soon after I moved into the flat when I was decorating the bathroom. I spilt some paint in the bath, and as I couldn't remove it any other way, I tried scraping it off with a knife." He gave a deprecating grin. "I got it off all right but scratched the bath in the process."

"Was it a new bath?"

"Yes, brand new. I had it installed when I took over the flat." That was the trouble, he couldn't say he had inherited a scratched bath from the previous tenant, since that particular lie could be nailed. "Have you found out anything else?" he asked anxiously.

Mr. Colbourne shook his head. "They've had one of the lab. people there, and have given the place a proper going-over, that's all I know."

The solicitor wore a pre-occupied air throughout the ensuing discussion, and Wise wondered if it was because his confidence in his client's innocence had been shaken.

"I hope you believe I'm innocent," he said diffidently during a pause.

"It doesn't matter what I believe," Mr. Colbourne replied in an austere tone. "My rôle is to see that everything is said on your behalf which you would say for yourself if you were versed in the rules of court procedure and evidence. A good lawyer does not become personally involved in his client's cause. Professionally, yes; personally, no."

Suppose I invited that little lecture, Wise reflected without pleasure. Serves me right for pretending to mind what someone thinks of me when all I care about is getting off the hook.

Mr. Colbourne removed his spectacles and gave them a vigorous polish. Without them his expression lost all its force, and his eyes blinked as if they had been suddenly abandoned. "At least the police can't have any evidence to justify a charge of capital murder," he said, putting his spectacles back on. "They can never prove, in the absence of a body or an admission, that Goodwin was shot rather than stabbed or strangled, nor that he was murdered in the course or furtherance of theft, though that will probably be a hidden inference."

"But I didn't murder him at all."

"I know. I'm only trying to see it from their angle."

Wise assumed an indignant air. "Are they going to try and suggest that I lured Mr. Goodwin to my flat in order to steal his wallet and that I then murdered him?"

"We shall have to wait until next week to know a lot of things," Mr. Colbourne replied unsatisfactorily. "But, as I say,

I don't think you need worry about capital murder. That means at worst you can only be sentenced to life imprisonment."

"I don't intend to be sentenced to anything," Wise declared, "I'm innocent."

15

If anything, Colin Wise found that his second week in prison passed more slowly than the first. There were letters from Lesley and further interviews with the principal medical officer, and twice a day for half an hour there was "exercise". Though Wise welcomed the release from the ward which it brought and enjoyed such fresh air as that part of South London ever knows, he found the actual shuffling progress which constituted exercise extremely degrading. It was like taking part in a badly organised protest march of the League of Corns and Bunions.

The only two bright features of his life were innumerable hot baths and the disappearance of Inky Pooler. The baths were attached to the ward, and since most of its occupants took no more than the obligatory one a week, there was never any run on them and the officers had no objection to Wise having one and sometimes even two a day. He didn't care what the rest thought, and was more amused than otherwise when Dr. Fleming questioned him about his habit. He didn't know if any interesting psychological significance could be read into excessive cleanliness, though he explained to the doctor that they represented a slice of home comfort and that the purely functional business of becoming clean was not a motivating factor.

Inky Pooler had gone off one morning to keep his tryst with the red judge at the Old Bailey, and Wise subsequently heard that he had been sent to some special mental institution. Given half a chance and a box of matches, he'd probably have it alight in no time at all.

And so eventually the day arrived for Wise to return to court. Once more there was the terrible and seemingly endless journey in the prison van, made so much the worse for not being able to see where you were going. But at last he was deposited, and the

123

red-faced sergeant conducted him to his cell with the air of a hotel porter escorting an habitual guest to his bedroom.

"You have it all to yourself today," he remarked, as he flung open the heavy wooden door and ushered Wise through. "And from the crowd outside, you're the biggest draw we've ever had. A good many of them'll get turned away, too. We'll have the 'house full' notices out before the curtain ever goes up. I hope you're flattered."

Wise made a face. "I imagine most of them have come only to stare."

"They get a kick out of listening to the things you've done and then looking at you and saying to themselves with lots of relish, 'Fancy, *he* did all that'."

"Except that I didn't."

"Doesn't matter, you're charged with murder and that's good enough for them. They'll believe you did it. No point in their coming otherwise."

"You're pretty cynical."

"So would you be if you'd had my job these last thirty years."

The sergeant, who was clearly in expansive mood, might have gone on indefinitely but for the arrival outside the cell door of Mr. Colbourne.

"We'll be starting in about twenty minutes," he said to Wise when the officer had ambled away.

"Anything further?" Wise asked anxiously.

Mr. Colbourne shook his head. "But we'll soon know the worst. Don't worry if I appear not to be asking the witnesses a lot of questions. The best tactic at the magisterial hearing is often to listen but not say much. Indeed, unless there's a chance of having the case chucked out for lack of evidence, it's best to reserve cross-examination until the trial. One of the advantages enjoyed by the defence is not having to disclose their case in advance, whereas the prosecution must."

This little speech from his solicitor gave Wise a disagreeable jolt. He had been looking to Mr. Colbourne to tear into the prosecution's case and leave it in shreds. Mr. Colbourne so brisk, self-assured and fearless. And yet here he was proposing to play an inactive rôle and talking about reserving cross-examination until the trial. For him it mightn't mean much, but for Wise it would involve further soul-destroying weeks in Brixton Prison. He burned with sudden hatred. He became aware that the solicitor was looking at him with an anxious expression and realised that his own face must have been reflecting his thoughts.

"I understand," he said coldly.

"My God, that look! I'd believe him capable of murdering anyone," Mr. Colbourne reflected with shock. He said, "I've brought you a pad of paper and I want you to note down any point that occurs to you as the prosecution develop their case. Remember, it's in the light of what we hear today that your defence is going to be finally moulded. Listen in particular for inconsistencies and for points which we can later rebut."

The solicitor departed, leaving Wise to await his own summons to court. This came five minutes later.

"You're on," the red-faced sergeant said, with aggressive jocularity, as he unlocked the cell door and motioned Wise to follow him.

The courtroom was packed, and if Wise had ever doubted his celebrity value since being charged with Goodwin's murder, the awesome hush which greeted his entry must have reassured him. The fact that he now ignored the crowded benches and declined to acknowledge their presence served only to increase the interest focused on his person. He might have been carved from stone as he stood motionless in the front of the dock staring ahead of him with a serious expression.

The lady chairman, in a fresh hat for the occasion, a black one which he hoped was of no significance, invited him to be seated. Mr. Colbourne sat forward with a studious frown and a virgin page of his notebook open before him.

When everyone was seated and most of the shuffling had died away, the clerk nodded at Mr. Hunt, who rose rather in the manner of a snake uncoiling itself. He was tall and thin, with shoulders hunched forward, and he had the serene expression of one who has ceased to be surprised by anything to which human nature can lend itself.

He glanced round, and for a second his eyes, grey and

125

unfathomable, met Wise's. Then he turned back and began his opening speech. His voice was pleasant and devoid of any emotion, and at first Wise found it uncanny that this lanky, middle-aged man, whom he'd never seen before, was telling everyone about him: who he was, where he came from and what he was supposed to have done. And all in a conversational tone as if he might have been describing a walking tour in the Lake District.

"What distinguishes this from most charges of murder which come before the courts," Mr. Hunt went on in his matter-of-fact way, "is the absence of a victim's body, for no trace has ever been found of Geoffrey Goodwin, the man who, the prosecution allege, has been murdered by this man in the dock." He made a vague gesture in Wise's direction as though to indicate whom he meant. "This is unusual but not unique, and it means that the prosecution must rely on circumstantial evidence to prove the fact of death. The prosecution must prove by such evidence not only that Goodwin is dead, but that he was murdered by this man here." Again the hand fluttered out toward Wise. "What is that evidence?"

The Press, Mr. Colbourne and Wise all perceptibly alerted their senses. The three magistrates' expressions remained masks of stolid interest.

"I have already told you something of the accused and of Goodwin and of this slightly unusual relationship between a television repair man and one of his employer's well-to-do clients —though I'm making no suggestion that there was anything improper in it—and it is against the background of that relationship that the evidence must be seen.

"On the evening of Friday, 20th March, Goodwin called at the accused's flat by arrangement for a social visit. The accused says he came primarily to see his, the accused's, drawings, which he had been wishing to view before he went away. He arrived in his car around eight o'clock and, according to the accused, stayed just over half an hour, before leaving once more in his car and alone." Mr. Hunt leaned forward and said with slow deliberation, "He was never seen again. So there is the first piece of evidence against the accused: he is the last known person to have seen Goodwin before he vanished without trace. But though Goodwin disappeared, his car did not. It was found the following Monday morning in the garage of his home, where Mr. Wright, a mechanic, went to fetch it. But Mr. Wright will tell you he found a number of unusual features when he arrived at Goodwin's cottage that Monday morning. In the first place, the key to the garage was in the lock although the arrangement had been that it would be left under a certain stone near the back door. Next, Mr. Wright found the car keys in the ignition slot when Mr. Goodwin normally always left them in one of the car pockets. Mr. Wright used to collect the car from Mr. Goodwin's home quite often, and he will tell you that this was the first time the garage key had not been left beneath the stone and the car keys were where he found them. The prosecution suggest that, whoever put the car away, it was not Mr. Goodwin, though clearly that was intended to be the presumption." Mr. Hunt hooked up one of his shoulders and went on in his mild tone. "But that's not all about the car. It's a Jaguar saloon, pale grey, registration number DBH 7843, and the prosecution will call evidence that such a car was seen not far from a canal from which the deceased's suitcases were recovered, just after midnight on the Saturday. Police-Constable Franklyn, who was cycling home, had his attention drawn to the car, and though it was travelling fast, he could see quite clearly that it was a pale-grey Jaguar and that its registration number was D something H with the figures 7, 4 and 3 following the letters." Mr. Hunt paused and turned a page of his notes while Wise had almost ceased to breathe in sickening dread of what was to come. "P.-C. Franklyn will tell you that there was only one person in the car and that was the driver. He will also tell you that the driver in no way resembled Goodwin, whose photograph he has seen." Mr. Hunt swung round and looked straight at Wise, who stared back at him without any outward sign of emotion. "He will tell you that the driver of Mr. Goodwin's Jaguar in the still hours of that Saturday night was somebody who in every way answers the description of the man in the dock."

Wise saw Mr. Colbourne make some heavy underlining of his notes and add a ferocious arrow in the margin. He rose and came across to Wise, who leaned over the edge of the dock to catch what he was whispering.

"Did this Franklyn ever pick you out on an identification parade?"

"No."

"Do you know who he is?"

"Not unless he was the constable who came into Superintendent Manton's office the first time I was taken to the station and who kept on staring at me. I certainly didn't know who he was."

Mr. Colbourne nodded with apparent satisfaction. "Anyway, I take it you weren't driving Mr. Goodwin's car near the canal on that Saturday night?"

"Never driven his car in my life."

Mr. Colbourne returned to his seat, leaving Wise feeling better. If he could not recognise the officer on the bicycle, he didn't see how the latter could possibly have recognised him, particularly since one would normally assume that the person in the car would stand a better chance of identifying a cyclist than the other way about. Bastards, he reflected grimly, fancy trying a trick like that! Well, just wait!

"And what, you may wonder," Mr. Hunt was going on, "was the car doing in that vicinity on that Saturday night? The prosecution allege that it was driven there by the accused to enable him to dispose of Mr. Goodwin's three suitcases and travel bag in the waters of the canal. You will hear from Detective-Superintendent Manton how those pieces of luggage, unmistakably Mr. Goodwin's, were recovered and how each had been perforated with holes the better to make them sink. Surely the recovery of Mr. Goodwin's luggage points as clearly as anything could that something sinister indeed had overtaken him. What other possible inference is there? Mrs. Paget, who was Goodwin's housekeeper, will tell you that he had completed his packing on the Friday morning while she was at the cottage, and that the suitcases were on the floor of his bedroom awaiting those few last-minute items that we never pack until the actual time for departure. And here again we find one of those small but highly significant clues which indicate that Goodwin never set off on

128

his journey, as we were obviously intended to believe—though if he had, why he should have discarded his luggage in a canal one can't even begin to speculate about. But supposing those suitcases had never been found, there was still this further discrepancy of behaviour to cast a doubt on the picture so cunningly left behind by the murderer."

Wise waited. Whatever was coming was what had first aroused Hilda's suspicions. He saw himself again standing in Goodwin's bedroom, looking around to see if he had forgotten anything before closing the suitcases and taking them out to the car.

"Mrs. Paget will tell you that Mr. Goodwin made several dozen trips during the time she knew him, and that on each of the trips he took with him a small leather Bible which he kept in the drawer of his bedside table. And yet on the Monday morning, following his supposed departure to Australia, when Mrs. Paget came to the cottage to clear up, she found the Bible still in the drawer. It was, she says, the last thing he would have left behind—and yet he did," Mr. Hunt added with quiet emphasis.

Though his expression gave nothing away, Wise inwardly cursed. He realised now that he should have acquainted himself better with the minor routine of Goodwin's every-day life. It was this unswerving adoption of routine which had created a great pit for Wise to fall into. Why couldn't Goodwin have been the sort of person who never put his car or garage keys twice in the same place and who had never packed to go away without something being left behind? But it was too late to lament what might have been, and in any event these small slips were still a long way from proving that Goodwin was dead, and even further that Wise had murdered him. Nevertheless, it was disturbing when he recalled the amount of thought and preparation he had given to the crime and how certain he had been beforehand that everything was accounted for.

Mr. Hunt's amiable tone continued with the prosecution's exposition of its evidence.

"As I say, the murderer, with cold, premeditated cunning, contrived to give the impression that his victim had left for Australia, and you may be wondering what evidence there is that Mr. Goodwin is not alive and well on the other side of the world. On the Saturday morning—he was booked to fly that afternoon—the B.O.A.C. counter at London Airport received a phone call from someone saying he was Mr. Goodwin and cancelling his reservation. This person, who the prosecution allege was the accused man, went on to tell a somewhat strange story about having to go over to Paris by boat and train—I would ask you to remember that piece of detail—and concluded the conversation by saying that he would pick up a flight in Rome, which is one of the airline's ports of call on its Australian route." Mr. Hunt held up his left hand with long, bony fingers outstretched, and with his right began to tick off the points he proceeded to enumerate. "Firstly, the prosecution can prove that no one by the name of Geoffrey Goodwin has arrived in Australia since his disappearance, and that those who were expecting him have waited in vain for any word to explain his failure to arrive. Secondly, that no one answering Goodwin's description has contacted any of B.O.A.C.'s offices in London, Paris, Rome, or anywhere else between here and Australia. Thirdly, that no one answering his description has ever registered his arrival in Paris. Fourthly, that none of those best qualified to know had any inkling of any proposed change in his plans, nor can they suggest any reason why he should have suddenly gone to Paris in this mysterious fashion. Fifthly, that he had never travelled to Paris by boat and train since the advent of the aeroplane."

With the final point Mr. Hunt reached his thumb. "You may think it clear, madam, that Goodwin never went to Australia, that he never went to Paris; in fact, that he has never left the shores of this country, for the reason that he is dead.

"As you may be aware, it is simpler to make an unnoticed exit from this country by cross-channel boat than it is by air, and that is why, the prosecution suggest, the person who telephoned B.O.A.C. saying he was Goodwin felt obliged to provide this elaborate and highly circumstantial tale. And as such it is but another instance of diabolical cunning on the part of the man who murdered Goodwin."

He turned over another page of his notes and gave his other shoulder a hitch while Wise silently awarded him full marks for deduction. In almost any other circumstances he felt he would have liked Mr. Hunt. The clinical, dispassionate manner, the quiet, steely competence and the aura of unflappability were attributes which would normally evoke his respect, even his envy, but being the object of their display was a less agreeable experience. He was particularly aware of becoming the cynosure of all eyes every time Mr. Hunt made one of his mildly emphasised points. Well, he couldn't prevent them staring, but they'd glean nothing; he wouldn't even flick an eyelash for them. They were so used to murderers who had made snivelling confessions long before they reached court that they were tantalisingly baffled by the enigma he posed in front of them. He would be interested to see what the Press made of him in their efforts to steer a course between contempt of court and the laws of defamation. Mr. Colbourne had discussed with him the question of an application for a hearing in camera. He opined that the magistrates would probably be prepared to accede to such a request, but that in a case as this, where the defence was a complete denial, the fullest pre-trial publicity might be more beneficial than otherwise in bringing forward witnesses who might be able to assist Wise's case. Wise, who had no particular feelings either way, readily agreed, though in a better position than Mr. Colbourne to know the improbability of anyone coming forward with any information useful to his defence.

"I now turn," Mr. Hunt went on, "to a piece of evidence of a different nature, though one of the utmost significance as being perhaps the most direct indication that Goodwin has not only been murdered, but that he was murdered in the accused's flat. I refer to certain marks found in the bath there." Mr. Hunt described the marks in considerable detail and concluded, "I shall be calling before you expert evidence to the effect that the marks are consistent with having been caused by a knife, a sharp knife. That they are the sort of marks which you would expect to find if someone had cut something up in the bath. The prosecution invite you to infer from all the circumstances that it was Goodwin's body which was dismembered in that bath. Dismembered and subsequently effectively disposed of."

Without moving his head, Wise let his eyes flick over the

faces he was able to see. Mr. Colbourne, with a studious frown, was bent over his notebook, every so often seizing a coloured pencil to mark a particular passage. The Press were scribbling away in their efforts to keep up with the trail being laid by the urbane Mr. Hunt. The three magistrates continued to look stolidly impassive, almost as though they were afraid that any movement, even to blow their noses, might be subject to mis-interpretation. Their clerk, slumped in his seat below the bench, had listened to Mr. Hunt with a faintly sceptical expression. From time to time he had cocked a mild eyebrow or pursed his lips in doubt and reached forward to make a scribbled note on a sheet of foolscap as if he were adding to a shopping list as fresh items occurred to him.

"The prosecution can offer you no direct evidence as to what happened to the deceased's body after death, though you may think it significant that the accused borrowed his employer's van that evening and returned it the following morning with both the outside *and* the inside washed and cleaned. He had given as his pretext for wishing to borrow it that he had a piece of furniture to pick up which he had bought in a sale. Now it happens that he had driven Mr. Gracey, his employer, home on that Friday evening, and Mr. Gracey had noticed what the mile-age reading was when he got out. When the van was returned on Saturday morning, Mr. Gracey observed that it had covered sixty-eight miles in the intervening period. He taxed the accused about this, who denied he had driven it that distance and firmly alleged that Mr. Gracey was mistaken." Mr. Hunt paused and raised a long, thin forefinger to emphasise what was coming. "But Mr. Gracey will tell you he is quite certain that he was not mistaken. And if he wasn't, what then is the inference? That, for some reason known only to him, the man in the dock has lied—and persisted in the lie, for he repeated it to the police—about the distance travelled by his employer's van that Friday night." Mr. Hunt appeared to fall into a study of the backs of his hands, then, slowly looking up, he said, "Of course, if the prosecution is right in saying that Goodwin was murdered in the flat, then Wise would have needed transport to remove the body. . . ."

The clerk, whose expression had become more sceptical during the last few minutes, heaved himself forward in his seat: "Forgive my interrupting you, Mr. Hunt, but as I understand what you've told the court, Mr. Goodwin's car would have been parked outside the accused's flat at this time?"

"That is so, sir."

"Then I don't quite follow why Mr. Gracey's van should have been put to the use you suggest if the deceased's own car was available?"

"The van would certainly have been more convenient, sir, for transporting a body."

The clerk looked unconvinced, and Mr. Hunt went on: "But, whichever way you care to speculate, the fact remains that the accused did borrow his employer's vehicle that evening. I am doing no more than pointing out the possible significance of that move."

The clerk gave Mr. Hunt a small, non-committal smile. "Since I have already interrupted you, I wonder if you would be so good as to deal with the question of motive before you conclude your opening. Perhaps," he added disarmingly, "I am anticipating what is about to come, but I know the magistrates would like to hear what you have to say on the subject."

Mr. Hunt cast his eyes down at his notes and ran a thoughtful finger across his mouth. Hadn't he spent a considerable amount of time discussing motive in conference with the heads of his own department and with the police? This was a case in which they had all recognised that the absence of a provable motive was an almost fatal flaw in the prosecution's case, just as by contrast the presence of a strong motive would clinch it. The failure of police inquiries to trace Peter Fox and the six thousand pounds he had apparently received from Goodwin, or to dig any deeper into that mysterious transaction, had been frustrating in the extreme. Here, they had felt, if they could only find out what had happened, lay the key to the whole matter.

"Without a motive we'll never hold him," Mr. Hunt had remarked to Manton on more than one occasion. And now here he was being invited to be specific about the very matter he had wished to gloss over.

He looked up from his papers. "The prosecution are not in a position to prove a motive in this case," he said in a quietly defiant tone. "But, having said that, I need hardly remind you that motive is not an essential element in the proof of a criminal charge under our law. Many a prisoner has been convicted without a motive for his crime having ever been established."

"Thank you," the clerk said politely. "I just wanted to know whether evidence of motive would be adduced."

Mr. Hunt looked at him steadily. "No, it will not," he repeated with a shake of his head. Shortly after this he concluded his opening, and for a few minutes there was an atmosphere of general post as most of the Press pushed their way out in search of telephones, and those who did remain wriggled about to ease their sore behinds.

Wise sat back and paid little attention to the first few witnesses, who consisted of police photographers and plan-drawers. Copies of their handiwork were passed up to him. There were plans both of his flat and of Goodwin's cottage. A fat album of photographs contained glossy prints of every room of the flat, and no fewer than six different views of the bath; also pictures of Mr. Gracey's van, Goodwin's car and garage, his water-logged suitcases, the stretch of the canal from which they had been recovered as seen by day and by night.

Wise turned back to the photographs of his own home and gazed at them with an anguished longing. It was hard to realise that it lay not much more than a mile distant, though for him now it could just as well be on the moon. And, anyway, how would it ever be the same after the police had been through it like a band of marauders? Not, of course, that he had intended to remain there long after Goodwin's death, and now he'd have every reason to clear out as soon as he was free. Go right away, change his name and feed on that six thousand pounds while he worked out the details of his next exploit, the wiser for his present experience. But the pictures of his home still filled him with distress in their reminder of the self-contained, independent existence from which he had been snatched. He recalled the deep satisfaction he felt every time he had let himself into his home and closed the front door behind him. It was a spiritual contentment he had never known before. His thoughts went to Patrick Fox. He regretted greatly the manner in which he had walked out on his blind friend, but he had no choice in the matter and was sure the old man understood. Patrick would know he was in trouble and he would leave it there. He had already declared his attitude during that nightmare confrontation at the police station. Wise hoped he would be able to do something for Fox in return, though it seemed likely that Peter Fox must needs have vanished as completely as Goodwin.

The police photographer vacated the witness-box and Mr. Hunt said, "I now call Mrs. Paget."

Poor Hilda, she looked bewildered and pathetically ill-at-ease as she repeated the oath after the clerk and then gave a little jump as Mr. Hunt began his questions.

"Do you know the man sitting in the dock?" he asked, after establishing her identity and occupation.

She looked around the courtroom with a puzzled expression.

"Colin, do you mean?" she asked hesitantly.

"This man, here?" Mr. Hunt said, with one of his delicate gestures.

"Colin. Yes, I know him." And she threw him a nervous but friendly smile. "Hello, Colin."

"You mustn't speak to him," Mr. Hunt admonished gently.

"He's in trouble, isn't he?" she asked with spirit. "Why shouldn't I try and cheer him up?"

A rustle of amusement went through the courtroom, and Wise smiled back at her gratefully.

Unruffled, Mr. Hunt had chosen to ignore the riposte. He now put a series of questions to her to elicit evidence of Colin Wise's visits to Goodwin's cottage, and of the mild friendship which had sprung up between the two men.

"Colin was always thoughtful and kind," she said. "He was a really nice boy and I used to enjoy his visits to the cottage. He and Mr. Goodwin used to discuss painting and things like that when he'd finished his work." She paused and before Mr. Hunt could ask his next question she blurted out, "I don't suppose I'm meant to say this, but no one'll ever persuade me he murdered Mr. Goodwin."

"No, you weren't," Mr. Hunt murmured resignedly.

"You must answer the questions you're asked and no more," the clerk said severely. "Your opinions are not evidence."

Mr. Colbourne had no questions to ask of Hilda when some fifteen minutes later she completed her evidence, and with a final smile of encouragement at Colin Wise she retired to the back of the court.

The next witness was Mr. Gracey, who, Wise noticed with malicious enjoyment, was going to sustain a crick in the neck rather than bring himself to look in the direction of the dock. Wise felt suddenly venomous towards him. He was a stupid, obstinate old bastard whom he had always held in mild contempt, and it was intolerable to see him standing in the witness-box cloaked in civic righteousness. Even if he was right about the mileage, how dare he cling to his obstinate belief in the light of Wise's plausible denial.

When he was questioned about the borrowing of the van and its return the next morning, it was clear from Mr. Hunt's persistence that Mr. Gracey was not coming fully up to proof.

"Who normally washed the van?"

"Wise."

"How often was it washed?"

"Depended."

"About how often?"

"Sometimes twice in one week and then not again for a fortnight. All depended, you see," he said uncomfortably.

"Was there a normal time and day for washing it?"

"It was usually done at the end of a day."

"Had you ever known it done first thing in the morning before?"

"Not that I can recall."

"Or on a Saturday morning?"

"Not that I can recall."

"So that this was unusual?"

Mr. Colbourne rose to his feet. "I don't know how much longer my learned friend intends to go on cross-examining his own witness. . . ."

Mr. Hunt gave him an unenthusiastic glance and returned his attention to the witness.

"How usual was it for the van to be washed on a Saturday morning?" he asked with an air of exaggerated patience.

"It was not usual."

"Thank you. And how usual was it for the interior of the van to be washed out?"

"It normally got a bit of a clean-out when the outside was being done."

"But you have told us that on this occasion the inside was thoroughly scrubbed?"

"Yes."

"Well, how often did it receive that sort of treatment?"

"Only once in a while."

"Thank you." Mr. Hunt sat down with an air of relief and Mr. Colbourne rose to his feet. They might have been operated by a single piece of mechanism, so co-ordinated was their movement.

"You wear spectacles, don't you, Mr. Gracey?"

"Not all the time."

"For reading?"

"Yes."

"For fine work?"

"Sometimes."

"Were you wearing your spectacles on either of the occasions you purport to have read the milometer—that is, on the Friday evening when Wise dropped you home or the next morning when you found him washing the van?"

"No, but I could read the mileage without my spectacles."

"The dashboard panel doesn't receive much light, does it?"

"I could read the figures all right."

"Will you answer my question please?" Mr. Colbourne said in a steely voice.

"I don't know what you mean by much light," Mr. Gracey replied.

"Is the court to understand that you don't wish to answer the question?"

The clerk intervened to rescue Mr. Gracey from the limb on

which he was uncomfortably perched. "Can we assume that the dashboard of your van is normally placed?"

"Yes."

The clerk turned to Mr. Colbourne. "I think you can leave the court to draw its own conclusions as to the amount of light there would be inside the van. We have a photograph of it in the album."

Mr. Colbourne gave a brisk nod of his head and returned his attention to the witness.

"Would you agree, Mr. Gracey, that it is not easy to distinguish between noughts and sixes and eights and nines on the milo-meter."

"Mightn't be for some."

"But even without your spectacles, you wouldn't experience any difficulty, is that what you're saying?"

"They're quite big figures," Mr. Gracey said defensively. "Much bigger than print in a book."

"Very well," Mr. Colbourne observed in a lawyer's favourite undermining tone and resumed his seat, leaving Mr. Gracey looking resentful and uncertain.

The next witness was P.-C. Franklyn, whom Wise immediately recognised as the constable who had come into Manton's office when he was there.

"Is that he?" Mr. Colbourne asked, stepping over to the dock.

"Yes."

Franklyn was a keen, clean-looking young officer with a pronounced adam's apple, which seemed to be working over-time as he took the oath in loud, emphatic tones. Under Mr. Hunt's questioning he described how he had been cycling home after midnight that Saturday when the Jaguar had passed him. He had given it more than normal attention since it wasn't usual to see a car on that particular road at that hour of the night and even less so a Jaguar.

"How many people were there in the car?" Mr. Hunt asked.

"One, sir. The driver."

"Would you recognise him if you were to see him again?"

"It was the accused, sir," he replied, pointing dramatically in Wise's direction.

Mr. Hunt and Mr. Colbourne performed their mutual bobbing act.

"What was the space of time between your first noticing the Jaguar and it passing from your view?" Mr. Colbourne asked.

"About half a minute, sir."

"During part of that time it would have been approaching you?"

"Yes, sir."

"With headlights on?"

"Yes, sir."

"So that during the period it was coming towards you you wouldn't have been able to read either the number plate or see how many people were in it?"

"I suppose not, sir."

"Suppose not?" Mr. Colbourne echoed severely.

"No, I wouldn't, sir."

"So that the only opportunity you had of seeing who was in the car was as it was passing you?"

"Yes, sir."

"Was there a street lamp anywhere in the vicinity?"

"No, sir, but it wasn't too dark a night."

"And I suppose it was after it had passed you that you tried to get the registration number?"

"Yes, sir."

Mr. Colbourne appeared to be thoughtfully weighing his next question, and Wise watched him intently. He had been doing fine; why had he stopped? But, unlike his client, Mr. Colbourne was aware that to cross-examine too far at this stage would be dangerous, that he ought not to do more than lay a foundation as he had done both with Mr. Gracey and the present witness. He decided, not without hesitation, to carry it a little further.

"Have you seen the accused between the time when you say you saw him driving the car and today?"

"Yes, sir."

"When was that?"

"In Detective-Superintendent Manton's office. I happened to go in there with some reports and the accused was sitting in the room and I recognised him."

"Were you expecting to see him in the room?"

"How do you mean, sir?"

"It's a perfectly simple question."

"No, I wasn't."

"It was a pure coincidence that you happened to enter when he was there?"

Franklyn's adam's apple plunged up and down as he swallowed twice. "Yes, sir. I was told to take some reports up to Mr. Manton—and I did."

"I see. Who told you?"

"Detective-Sergeant Grant, sir."

"You're not a member of the C.I.D.?"

"No, sir."

"Do you know why you were selected for this particular duty?"

"No, sir. I just happened to be available, I suppose."

"Do you often run errands for the C.I.D.?"

"No, sir."

"How many officers—perhaps I should say constables—would there have been on duty at the station that evening?"

"I've no idea, sir."

"A dozen, two dozen, fifty?"

"I can't say, sir."

"But the fact remains that it was you who was sent along to Mr. Manton's room?"

"Yes, sir."

Mr. Colbourne sat down, to P.-C. Franklyn's apparent relief.

Bloody liar! Wise thought. How could he possibly have recognised me! Like Mr. Gracey, he had deserved the roasting Mr. Colbourne had given him, though why in each case had the solicitor not torn even further into their fabrications? Well, not exactly fabrications perhaps, but certainly guesswork. And as for Franklyn's confrontation with him in Manton's office, that could now be seen as a put-up job of the most cynical kind. Wise felt indignant that he had been made the victim of such dishonest practice.

A rapid succession of witnesses passed in and out of the box, each fitting a small piece of the prosecution's case into place.

Wise knew none of them and had indeed been wholly unaware of their existences until they stepped into the court-room. They for their part were plainly curious to have a good look at the man who was the cause of their having travelled, in several cases considerable distances, to give their evidence. Wise stared coldly back at them until, embarrassed, they shifted their gaze. Their evidence was mostly brief, and Mr. Colbourne invariably said a brisk "cross-examination reserved" when Mr. Hunt sat down after his examination-in-chief.

By the end of the day twenty-three witnesses had been called and Mr. Hunt indicated that he had six more, including scientific and police officers. The lady chairman announced an adjournment until the next morning, and Wise was shepherded to the cells, where Mr. Colbourne came to see him before he was taken back to Brixton.

"How do you think it's gone?" Wise asked anxiously.

"I'm not dissatisfied."

"I noticed that you didn't ask any questions of the later witnesses."

"There was no point in doing so. The effect of their evidence, which was a series of negatives, was supposedly to show that Goodwin must be dead. That's a matter of inference which we'll dispute when the time comes. Indiscriminate cross-examination of those witnesses wouldn't have helped us in any way. Also don't forget that your defence is that, whatever's happened to Goodwin, you've had nothing to do with it."

"That's true."

"It's not for us to prove what's happened to him. It's for the prosecution to prove two things: firstly that he's dead, secondly that it was you who killed him."

"And you think we're doing all right?"

"The prosecution has not sprung any surprises and we can be grateful for that. Hunt knows as well as anyone that his case is full of loopholes and I think we've been able to widen one or two of them."

Wise was disconcerted by Mr. Colbourne's apparent assumption that the loopholes were an indication of the prosecution's failure to dig up evidence rather than of his client's innocence.

He had learnt, however, not to try to persuade his solicitor by any emotional plea that he was innocent of the charge. Mr. Colbourne's approach was strictly legal and wholly objective.

"What'll happen when the evidence is finished?"

"I shall have to decide whether or not it's worth while my making a submission of no case to answer. That means, asking the magistrates to dismiss the charge."

"So that I'd be free?"

"Yes, but don't raise your hopes, because I doubt whether they'll accept the responsibility. It's asking a lot in a murder case, and it isn't difficult for them to satisfy themselves that there's some evidence to be considered by a jury. However, it may even so be a good thing to make a submission. We'll see how it goes tomorrow."

"I hope you will try to get me off here," Wise said desperately.

"I've explained there's not much hope." Mr. Colbourne's tone was edgy.

Wise took a deep breath. "Look, sir," he said, "every day I spend in prison feels like a year. I don't want to remain there a minute longer than I have to. I'm innocent and I want to be free. I'm very grateful to you for all you're doing, but I'm not sure whether you realise what hell it is being shut up all day. I want to get out, I still have normal feelings and emotions. I'm still a person, even though I have been given a number. From the way people stared at me in court all day, you'd never think I was made of the same flesh and blood as them. But I am, sir."

Mr. Colbourne was silent for several seconds, while Wise searched his face in vain for a clue as to what he was thinking. At length he said, "Very well, I'll make a submission, but—and I repeat but—don't let it raise too many hopes in your mind." He turned to go. "I'll see you in the morning."

Wise scarcely slept that night. The prospect, however remote, of being freed the next day was one which his mind remorselessly gnawed at as he lay on his hard, narrow bed in the hospital ward.

The scene, however, as the court settled down the next morning was so unchanged that he had the impression there had been no break in the proceedings. The lady chairman was wearing the same hat and the same solemn expression, and her two male companions gave the appearance of having no existence beyond the confines of the court-room. The clerk, Mr. Hunt and Mr. Colbourne looked precisely as they had when the case had been adjourned the previous evening.

Wise could feel his hopes and anxieties becoming smothered, and struggled to prevent himself being totally engulfed by the insidious atmosphere of unreality. It was as if the proceedings and the way they were conducted were more important than their object.

The first witness was Detective-Sergeant Chester, who managed to sound disagreeable even when taking the oath. He described his visit to Wise's home in the company of Detective-Constable Brook, and in a voice laden with innuendo referred to the marks found in the bath.

"Did you invite the accused's explanation of them?" asked Mr. Hunt.

"I did not, sir. I had no intention of letting the accused know what I had observed."

"And later did you go into the garage?"

"I did."

"Did you notice whether there were any marks on the floor?"

"There were none. The floor looked as though it had been recently cleaned. I drew the accused's attention to this and he agreed that it had."

When Mr. Colbourne rose to cross-examine, he demanded severely, "You want to make your evidence sound more significant than it is, don't you?"

"That's not a proper question," Mr. Hunt rejoined in a mild tone.

"Perhaps it is more a matter of comment," Mr. Colbourne agreed and sat down again. He hadn't any questions he really wished to ask but had wanted to underline his rejection of Sergeant Chester's evidence. The officer glared at him angrily.

After D.-C. Brook, who was the next witness, there came Mr. Vallett of the Metropolitan Police Laboratory. At the same time a murmur of excited interest rippled through the court as two plain-clothes' officers carried the bath in.

The witness gave an account of a visit to Wise's flat with the air of one who spent his life examining people's baths and plumbing. Wise listened with growing apprehension and resentment, which finally turned to relief when it became clear that nothing more damning than the marks themselves was forthcoming.

"Let us get the drains out of the way first," Mr. Colbourne said energetically, as he stood up to cross-examine. "Is it correct that your examination of the bath waste-pipe and of the drain into which it empties revealed nothing to suggest that a body had been cut up in the bath?"

"That is so, but——"

"Thank you; I don't want any 'buts', you have answered my question."

"The witness is entitled to qualify his reply," Mr. Hunt demurred.

"What were you going to add?" asked the clerk.

"Only that if the bath had been well washed down afterwards and water had been allowed to flow freely through the waste pipe, one wouldn't necessarily expect to find traces left behind."

"Would it not have been probable for, say, splinters of bone to have become lodged in the U-bend of the waste pipe if a body had been dismembered in the bath?"

"That would certainly have been possible."

"You had it in mind when you examined the pipes?"

"I did."

"But found nothing?"

"I found nothing at all of that nature," Mr. Vallett said in an almost apologetic tone.

"I'd now like to ask you about the marks in the bath. You have told the court there were two types. One consistent with the point of a knife having, as you put it, overshot its run and so to speak stabbing the side of the bath. The other being scratches on the bottom of the bath, which you suggest were caused by the blade of a sharp knife, as opposed to its point." Mr. Colbourne paused and the witness gave an attentive nod. "You're not suggesting that these marks could not have been caused in some other way?"

"I obviously can't."

"Supposing someone had been trying to scrape off paint which had been spilled on to the sides and bottom of the bath, could the marks not have been caused in that fashion?"

Mr. Vallett pursed his lips and sought inspiration in the ceiling. "It would depend what the person was using to scrape with," he said at length.

"A knife."

The witness cogitated again. "I wouldn't have expected scraping to have caused the sort of marks I found."

"But you couldn't exclude that as a possible explanation?"

"Exclude? No. But it's less likely than the explanation I've given."

Mr. Colbourne sat down, and Wise leant back in his chair with satisfaction.

The succeeding witnesses brought with them an air of anti-climax. By now both Press and public were becoming bored with all the detail, much of it indeed tedious and seemingly far removed from the starkness of murder. They were impatient for the end: impatient to know how it would be resolved even though this was not an Old Bailey trial with its climactic moment of a jury's verdict.

The final witness was Manton, in dark suit, chaste tie and stiff white collar. With his fair hair, thinning slightly in front, brushed back, and his strikingly blue eyes and healthily tanned complexion, he looked more like a ski-ing instructor dressed for the city than a detective-superintendent of the Metropolitan Police. For quiet urbanity, however, he matched Mr. Hunt, who now proceeded to elicit his evidence in the enervating atmosphere of mid-afternoon.

Wise listened with concentrated attention, ready to pounce on any distortions of the truth and convey them to his solicitor's notice.

"From first to last has Wise denied the charge?" Mr. Colbourne demanded when his turn came.

"He has."

"And indeed having any knowledge of what has happened to Goodwin?"

"That is so."

"You found none of Wise's fingerprints on Goodwin's car?"

"No. The only prints were those of Mr. Goodwin. At least they match others found in his cottage and are assumed to be his."

"I take it that no efforts have been spared to try to find Goodwin?"

"I think we've done everything we could."

"Without success?"

"So far."

"You mean that endeavours are still continuing?"

"Whenever we obtain a fresh lead we follow it up."

"Have your inquiries shown that Goodwin has previously gone away without warning?"

"He did on one occasion."

"Will you tell the court about that?"

"I understand, madam," Manton said, turning to the chairman, "that about three years ago he went to France without telling anyone that he was going."

"Was that in connection with a writing assignment?"

"So I understand." In a quiet but deadly tone he then added, "But on that occasion he was away only three days."

Mr. Colbourne showed no outward sign of being dismayed by the answer but nevertheless passed abruptly to a different topic.

"Is it true to say that you have uncovered no motive against Wise for the crime with which he has been charged?"

This was a taunting question which made Manton bite his tongue. He would dearly like to have replied that he most strongly suspected Wise to be Peter Fox and the cheque for six thousand pounds to be a fraud of some sort. (It said much for Wise's skill that it had not been detected as a forgery, though this in any event was almost impossible to prove without Goodwin's evidence.) But Manton saw no hope of converting his suspicions into proof. God knows he had worked hard enough at this aspect of the case. He glanced across at Wise sitting composedly in the dock. The police might possess all the weapons of criminal investigation, but Wise had got off to a good start and they weren't going to catch him.

Manton looked back at Mr. Colbourne and said impassively, "There is no evidence of a motive in this case." Only a faint emphasis on the word *evidence* indicated his feelings.

"That is the case for the prosecution," Mr. Hunt declared, as Manton departed from the witness-box.

Mr. Colbourne was on his feet again. "I wish to make a submission of no case to answer, madam."

The magistrates looked nonplussed while others in court wriggled into fresh postures.

"You may think," Mr. Colbourne began, "that the prosecution's case is just about as flimsy as any you have ever heard in support of a criminal charge. A man has mysteriously disappeared and a number of random clues tend to show that he didn't leave for Australia as he had planned. Some marks are found in my client's bath—and I wonder how many of us don't have marks of one sort or another in our baths—and it is suggested that the man's body must have been cut up there, principally, as I follow the evidence, because of the precedent suggestion that Wise was the last person to have seen the man. Have you ever heard wilder deduction than that in a court of law? The vanished man's suitcases are recovered from a canal which may add to the mystery of his disappearance but do nothing to add to the case against my client. Indeed, the only piece of evidence which does touch him directly is that of P.C. Franklyn, who on a dark night and with an opportunity measured in split seconds purports to be able to see the driver of Goodwin's car, so that when he later—and we are expected to believe quite fortuitously—sees Wise in Mr. Manton's office, he immediately recognises him as the man who was driving the Jaguar." Mr. Colbourne's eyes flashed indignantly. "I ask you to say that P.C. Franklyn's evidence is completely unreliable and unworthy of belief."

Mr. Colbourne now went on to pass judgment on each of the witnesses in turn, including Detective-Sergeant Chester, whom he designated as someone who could make a field of turnips sound suspicious.

"I ask you, madam," he concluded in a ringing tone, "to accept your responsibilities and to say that there is no evidence on which a jury acting reasonably could convict and accordingly to dismiss the charge." He sat down abruptly and ran a wiping hand across his forehead.

Wise looked expectantly toward the magistrates, who had gone into a huddle with their clerk. How could they possibly commit him for trial after that? Mr. Colbourne had been magnificent; even the Press had ceased to look bored.

The solicitor came across and stood beside the dock. Wise greeted him with a nervous smile.

"Surely. . . ?"

Mr. Colbourne made a doubtful face. "Don't rely on it."

There was a stir on the bench, somebody called out "Stand", and the magistrates disappeared through their door.

"Well, at least they're going to consider it," Mr. Colbourne observed.

Wise was taken back to his cell. He sat down, closed his eyes and tried to deflect his mind from the only subject on which it wished to dwell. He tried imagining he was somewhere else, in a station waiting-room, in a boat alone on a lake, in a lift going to the top of a high building.

He heard the door being unlocked and opened his eyes. "They're ready," the fat, red-faced sergeant said.

Wise stood up and squared his shoulders. "What do you think my chances are?"

The officer gave a mirthless laugh. "Nil."

A few minutes later they heard the lady chairman announce with unemotional stolidity, "We find there is a case to answer."

16

Colin Wise was committed for trial at the June session of the Central Criminal Court and taken back to Brixton Prison to await the day three weeks ahead. Mr. Colbourne, who had visited him in the court cell immediately after the conclusion of the magisterial proceedings, had attempted to bolster his spirits by saying that they wouldn't have a day too many for a proper preparation of the defence.

"I told you not to let your hopes be raised. I'll be along to see you in a few days' time. Meanwhile, I want you to write down any further points which occur to you, thinking back over the hearing, and we'll discuss them when I come. I'll now get down to preparing a proof of your evidence which we'll want to go through carefully together."

Wise lifted his gaze from the floor, which he had been staring at in concentrated gloom. "My evidence is very short. I haven't murdered Mr. Goodwin and I have no idea what's happened to him. I can't say anything further."

"Nevertheless counsel will require something more," Mr. Colbourne replied drily. "Incidentally, it'd be as well to have a word about counsel now. I want to retain them as soon as possible. The magistrates granted you a defence certificate for two, which means a Q.C. and a junior barrister can be briefed to defend you. Have you any preference?" Wise shook his head. Mr. Colbourne could suggest a couple of road sweepers and he'd not be any the wiser. "In that event I suggest Mr. Francis Milroy and Mr. Gavin Trend."

"Which is the Q.C.?"

"Mr. Milroy. Do you mean you've never heard of him?"

"No. Why should I have?"

149

"His name's always in the newspapers. He has a fine record for successful defences in criminal trials."

"O.K. If you recommend them, I'll agree. How old are they?"

"Mr. Milroy is around fifty and Mr. Trend about ten years younger."

"And you're sure they're the best?"

A note of asperity entered Mr. Colbourne's tone. "I wouldn't otherwise have suggested them. We must hope they'll be able to accept the briefs. They are both very busy men."

"I'm sorry, I didn't intend to sound critical, but this all means rather more to me than it does to you and the two gentlemen you mention. And that's not meant to be critical either. But I'm just another case to you lawyers: to myself I'm the only thing that matters at this particular moment."

Mr. Colbourne seemed to be weighing his answer with some care, and Wise prepared for a rebuke. In an almost curt tone the solicitor said, "Perhaps it'll make you feel happier if I tell you that shortly after I'd qualified I began to go blind in both eyes. I felt much as you do now when my own doctor recommended a specialist who also happened to be one of the busiest men in London with hundreds of patients on his books. But I went to him and he saved my sight." Mr. Colbourne didn't wait for Wise's reaction but turned and went as he finished his little parable.

Back in Brixton, prison life resumed its treadmill routine. Wise didn't mix much with the others in the ward but kept himself to himself. He managed to do this without giving the impression of being arrogant or stuck-up, and indeed such phrases as "quiet and well-behaved", "reserved but polite when spoken to" and "gives no trouble at all" provided the recurring theme in the log kept by the hospital officers.

He had a number of lengthy interviews with the Principal Medical Officer and came rather to enjoy these sessions in the small, cosy office on the ground floor of the hospital block.

"Have you been in touch with my foster-parents, sir?" he asked on one occasion.

"As a matter of fact, I have."

"They didn't want to come and see me?"

150

"I told them you didn't wish to be visited."

"I expect they were relieved."

"Possibly."

After one of these interviews, the doctor made a note which read, "No sign of any mental disorder. Certainly fit to plead and stand his trial. If he did all that is alleged against him, which, of course, he completely denies, he presents a clinical picture of a dangerous, amoral young man to whom killing is a means to an end rather than an end in itself. His composure is remarkable, and he knows how to make himself likeable. But even if he did commit the crime with which he is charged, my report must be the same. Neither Macnaughton Rules insane nor suffering from diminished responsibility."

Letters from Lesley continued to reach Wise on an average of every three days. They were repetitious and he was thankful to be absolved from answering them, though he still pondered whether to make use of the girl as a witness. He finally decided against such a course after a visit from one of Mr. Colbourne's clerks. The interview had reached an end, and the clerk was about to depart, when he remarked, "I reckon you have a better chance of getting off than any of the other poor sods in this prison who are awaiting trial."

"You mean that?"

"I really do. Even Mr. Colbourne thinks you'll be acquitted, and he's not given to optimistic forecasts. The prosecution's case is paper thin and you haven't made any admissions."

"I've not made any because I didn't do it," Wise replied. He was determined to protest his innocence on every occasion that doubt was cast upon it.

"You should make a good witness, too," the clerk went on as though appraising the qualities of a horse in the saddling enclosure.

"It doesn't matter not having any witnesses to speak for me?"

"Witnesses can be a liability—sometimes. Anyway, we want Mr. Milroy to have the last word."

The clerk went on to explain that where the defence called no witnesses other than the accused, their counsel made his speech

151

after that of the prosecution. But that if other witnesses were called, then the prosecution had the final word.

"When shall I see Mr. Milroy and the other barrister?"

"Probably not before you get to the Old Bailey. But don't worry, Mr. Colbourne will have attended consultations with them and we'll have your defence really jacked up by the time you reach court."

"You mean they won't come and see me here?" Wise asked with surprise.

"They might do, but it's not usual. Anything they want by way of further instructions Mr. Colbourne will attend to. That's the way it works," he added breezily.

"Well, please tell Mr. Colbourne I'd like to meet them before I go on trial," Wise said firmly. "Remind him that he met the surgeon before he had his operation." The clerk looked mystified. "He'll know what I mean."

Two days before his trial his wish was granted, and he received a visit in prison from his counsel and solicitor. Mr. Colbourne's clerk came the day before, apparently for the express purpose of informing him of the honour about to be bestowed, and then the next afternoon he was escorted over to the now familiar block and shown into one of the drearily decorated interview rooms. The two men with Mr. Colbourne looked up with frank interest as he entered.

"Wise, this is Mr. Milroy, who is leading for the defence, and this is Mr. Trend, his junior," Mr. Colbourne announced in a semi-awed voice. They each shook hands with Wise.

Mr. Milroy had rugged features, black wiry hair and wore horn-rimmed spectacles. He was thin and not particularly tall and in no way resembled Wise's mental picture of a Q.C. other than in his dress. Nor, for that matter, did Mr. Trend, who was over six feet tall and must have weighed nearly twenty stone. He was topped by unkempt hair which had no parting and stuck up at the back. His expression, however, was of someone who was always expecting to be amused.

Mr. Milroy leaned back against the edge of the table. "Well, Wise, I've read the papers and I think you have a reasonable run." It was several seconds before Wise realised that it was not the newspapers which were being referred to. The solicitor himself nodded sagely and gave Wise the sort of look he might have bestowed on a child whose conduct was open to doubt. Mr. Milroy went on, "Mr. Trend agrees with me"—it was Mr. Trend's turn to nod—"and, moreover, we're fortunate in that the case'll be tried before a good judge, Mr. Justice Raven. The defence couldn't wish for a better one." Mr. Trend and Mr. Colbourne again both nodded gravely as Mr. Milroy turned to them for endorsement of this view.

"How long do you reckon it'll last, sir?" Wise asked.

"Say three or four days, the judge is no time-waster, and I think I may reasonably claim that I'm not either. But speeches and summing-up, not to mention evidence, all take time, and prosecuting counsel will, I imagine, spend a fair while cross-examining you. You must be ready for that."

"What sort of questions will he ask?"

"He'll do his best to find a chink in your evidence and then exploit it. Incidentally, it'll be Mr. Brown, one of the Senior Treasury Counsel. He's fair, mind you, but that doesn't mean he'll pull his punches."

"I can only stick to the truth," Wise said in a quiet voice. "I've already told Mr. Colbourne all I know." He met Mr. Milroy's appraising gaze. "Do you really believe Mr. Goodwin's dead, sir?"

"I don't think the prosecution's evidence is very strong on that point. On the other hand, it's enough to make a jury wonder what's happened to him. And it's always dangerous to give them ground for morbid speculation." He turned to Mr. Colbourne. "I take it you've had no luck turning up anything which might show that Goodwin has suffered from loss of memory or blackouts in the past?"

"I'm afraid not. He always seems to have enjoyed excellent health."

"Pity." He glanced over the top of his spectacles at Mr. Trend. "Have you got anything to add, Gavin?"

"Only this. I think Wise must be prepared to hear the prosecution hammer at the somewhat unusual relationship which existed between Goodwin and himself. They're bound to shove it under the jury's nose and say in effect, 'Even though we're unable to prove a motive in this case, there was obviously something fishy between these two, and your guess is as good as anyone's.'"

"But there was nothing fishy between us at all," Wise said indignantly.

Mr. Trend gave him an unperturbed smile. "I'm only saying how the relationship can be made to appear from outside. Its unconventionality plus the fact that you were the last person to see Goodwin is bound to excite speculation, and, as Mr. Milroy has just said, that's not good for a jury."

"But how can anyone in their right mind suggest that there was anything mysterious in our relationship? I'm not a queer, if that's what you mean, and neither was Mr. Goodwin so far as I was aware. It was just that we both happened to be interested in art and he wanted to come and see some of my work before he went away."

Mr. Trend sighed. "I dare say, but it's as well that you should be alive to the sort of subtle hints which may be edged in the jury's direction. The prosecution will naturally stress that it's not part of their job to prove a motive, but at the same time they'll realise better than most that juries like to be supplied with a motive and never more so than in a case such as this."

Mr. Trend, who had been talking with his head propped up by a hand cupped beneath his chin, now fanned his fingers across his mouth and yawned through them.

"Anything you want to ask us, Wise, before we go?" Mr. Milroy inquired.

There was. He wanted to know if they really believed him innocent and what they would do to help him if things went desperately wrong. It was awful having to rely so completely on other people. How could they possibly feel as he did? The chilling answer was that they couldn't and didn't, and he realised that any attempt to extract further words from which to distil comfort were more likely to achieve the opposite effect. They were not concerned in giving him comfort, only in safeguarding their own reputations as delphic oracles.

"I don't think so, sir."

"Then we'll be seeing you at court the day after tomorrow."
He picked up his black homburg and moved to the door.
"Incidentally, you may like to know that the prison medical
officer has given you a clean bill of health."

"I don't see what else he could have done," Wise remarked.

An officer came along the passage as soon as the door began
to open. One might have thought, Wise reflected viciously,
that I was going to try and escape, disguised as a lawyer.

His three legal advisers were silent until they reached their
car, parked outside the main gate.

"Well, Gavin, what do you make of our chap now you've
seen him?" Mr. Milroy asked.

"He's either innocent or the coolest murderer I've ever met."

"But which?"

"I think he's probably guilty."

"I don't! I believe this is one of those rare cases where out-
rageous fortune has ensnared an innocent victim."

"But what about Franklyn's identification of Wise?" Mr.
Colbourne asked earnestly.

Mr. Milroy made a scoffing sound. "Not worth the mud
on a policeman's boots. I guarantee Franklyn would never have
picked him out on a properly conducted parade. That was a real
fix. They were after Wise and everything had to be made to fit
the theory they'd already formed. It isn't the first time the police
have done that. Anyway, Gavin, if you think he's guilty, you
must have some idea as to motive?"

"Could be what I obliquely suggested."

"Homosexual? Not the slightest evidence."

"They were both bachelors."

Mr. Milroy laughed. "Don't be so naïve, Gavin."

"Of course, the police believe the motive's tied up with the
six thousand pounds which was mysteriously drawn out of
Goodwin's bank account shortly before his disappearance," Mr.
Colbourne said. "Hunt, the Director's representative, told me
that off the record."

"There isn't the slightest evidence our chap ever received
six thousand pounds or any part of it. He has less than a hundred
pounds in his bank account." Mr. Milroy manœuvred the car

into the main traffic on Brixton Hill. "No, I was struck by him, and I think he'll make a good impression in the box."

"Oh, I think he'll do that all right," Mr. Trend remarked.

Mr. Milroy accelerated past a bus. "I reckon we have an excellent chance."

"Oh, so do I," Mr. Trend agreed.

"He should certainly be acquitted on that evidence," Mr. Colbourne contributed in a judicial tone.

They drove on in silence. Meanwhile, the object of their surmise lay on his bed and allowed his mind to dwell dreamily on a new life with six thousand pounds in his pocket.

17

Halfway up the sharp narrow staircase one of the prison officers turned and motioned Wise to wait while he himself mounted to the top and looked around him like a sailor who has shinned up the mast. Colin Wise, for his part, felt as though he was standing at the bottom of a well. He could see nothing apart from a glass roof high over his head. He leaned against the wall and glanced at the other officer who shared the step with him and who wore the expression of one who knew he was in for a boring day. He was picking his teeth industriously with a match-stick.

From somewhere overhead came the sound of three muffled knocks, and immediately the murmur of voices died away to be replaced by the scraping of feet.

"What's happening?" Wise asked.

"Judge," the officer replied round the edge of the toothpick.

Wise heard a voice intoning something, followed by more scuffing sounds and then the officer at the top of the steps beckoned to him.

He would never forget that first ascent into Number One Court at the Old Bailey—as bit by bit it came into view until he was standing at the front of the vast dock and gazing across a small chasm at the judge and a number of prosperous-looking men in dark-blue, fur-trimmed gowns. But it was the bright scarlet of the judge's robe with its broad white ermine cuffs that transfixed and held his eye. This was Inky Pooler's red judge all right. By contrast all else appeared drab. The buff walls, the dark suits, the rows of black-gowned barristers might have been designed so as not to deflect attention from the figure in flaming scarlet.

Wise became aware that the clerk of the court was addressing him. "Not guilty," he said in a quiet but firm tone in answer to the formal question which was asked of him.

The clerk now proceeded to inform him that the jury was about to be sworn and that if he wished to object to any of them he must do so before they took the oath. He glanced down at Mr. Milroy, who was sitting back with arms folded and a serene expression. Mr. Trend sat immediately behind him, Mr. Colbourne in front at a large table in the well of the court, which was under Wise's nose.

Nobody had said anything to him, but Wise assumed he wasn't supposed to denounce any of the twelve already sitting in the box and waiting to be sworn. There were two women amongst them, motherly-looking types. That was good. He'd always got on well with middle-aged females and he couldn't believe they would let him be convicted. As for the remaining ten jurors, they were, apart from two, a nondescript bunch of mixed ages and occupations from their appearances. The couple who claimed his attention were a large, bad-tempered looking man with receding grey hair and, one away from him, a man with a small, pursed mouth, who wore gold-rimmed spectacles. In addition, this man's hair was parted in the centre, and Wise had always viewed with suspicion anyone who sported this fashion. In his experience they were either daft or bigoted, and this man was plainly not daft.

One by one the jurors clutched the card which was handed them in turn, and in tremulous, faltering tones read out the words of the oath. The only exceptions were the two men Wise had already noticed. The sour-faced man took the oath in a clear, ringing voice and the other in high-pitched but fluent tones. When they were all sworn, the clerk completed the formalities, and Mr. Justice Raven, who had been sitting listening with a detached air, now peered down at the barrister sitting at the opposite end of the row to Mr. Milroy and said, "Yes, Mr. Brown."

"May it please your lordship. Members of the Jury, I appear in this case with my learned friend Mr. Fisher for the Crown and the accused man is represented by my learned friends Mr.

Milroy and Mr. Trend." Mr. Brown gave his gown a hitch and plunged into the narrative of his opening speech.

To Wise it sounded little different from what Mr. Hunt had expounded to the magistrates, and since, moreover, the jurors had undoubtedly read full accounts of the case in the newspapers, it all seemed a bit unnecessary. It was almost as if Mr. Brown read his thoughts, for he now went on, "Members of the jury, this case has already attracted wide publicity and it would be idle for me to imagine that you approach it with fresh minds— and yet that is precisely what you must do. As my lord will remind you at a later stage, you must try the accused solely on the evidence which you hear in this court today and on succeeding days. You must banish from your minds everything you may have read about the case before you stepped into that jury box a few minutes ago. . . ."

Wise had no way of knowing whether what they had previously read would dispose them in his favour or otherwise. He could only hope, but it did strike him as silly that anyone could imagine that minds could be wiped clean like slates. He glanced across at the judge, who was leaning back in his large leather-backed chair and listening with a relaxed expression. He certainly didn't look like the sort of man who would smack his lips as he sentenced prisoners, which was Colin Wise's preconceived image of how every judge would appear. His glance travelled on to the jury, who, at this early stage, were sitting like attentive school-children. Only the sour-faced man wore a bored, sceptical expression, and, as Wise was later to observe, this never left his face. In the rows behind counsel sat a number of elegantly dressed men and women. Above them the public gallery was packed with a gawking throng, some of whom he later learnt had queued as much as six hours to make sure of a seat. He recognised in the Press box a number of the same faces which had followed his fortunes through the magisterial hearing. Tonight nothing short of a major political assassination would keep his story from the front pages of the evening papers.

All the while he glanced covertly about him he continued to listen to Mr. Brown, who spoke in a dry, unemotional tone, and, as it seemed to Wise, without great enthusiasm for his cause. By the time he had finished emphasising that the burden of proving the charge lay on the prosecution and that the accused was entitled to be acquitted in default of its discharge, Colin Wise's hopes were higher than they had been since his arrest. Mr. Brown concluded his opening and sat down.

The first few witnesses brought no drama with their evidence and merely repeated the testimony they had given in the lower court. Hilda, who threw Wise a warm smile as she came into court, was the first witness to be cross-examined at any length by Mr. Milroy.

"Did you ever notice anything unusual between Mr. Goodwin and the accused?"

"I don't know what you mean, sir."

"Nor do I, Mr. Milroy," the judge added drily.

"Did it ever strike you as a curious relationship?"

"In what way?"

"In any way?"

"No."

"You see, it has been suggested that people in Mr. Goodwin's position are not usually friendly with those like the accused. What do you say about that?"

"Mr. Goodwin was friendly with everyone, sir. He used to enjoy talking to all different sorts of people. Said it was all part of his job as an author."

"Thank you, Mrs. Paget."

Hilda turned to go, when the judge addressed her. "Tell me, Mrs. Paget," he said pleasantly, "do you have personal knowledge of any occasion when your employer went to the accused's flat?"

"Oh no, sir."

"Did you know Mr. Goodwin was proposing to visit the accused on the evening before his departure for Australia?"

"No, sir."

The judge nodded at counsel to indicate he had finished, and Hilda was replaced by the next witness.

It was afternoon before Mr. Gracey gave evidence. On seeing him again, Wise found it difficult to mask the venom he felt

towards his erstwhile employer. Most of all it was his air of
quiet, self-righteous citizenship which incensed Wise. He wanted
to see him humbled and mortified, the target of judicial scorn
and of public derision. Unfortunately, however, he incurred
neither, and in the eyes of most onlookers Mr. Gracey might
be said to comport himself with inoffensive dignity. At length
Mr. Milroy rose to cross-examine and Wise sat forward in eager
anticipation of the lethal thrust.

"It's correct, isn't it, Mr. Gracey, that you were not wearing
your spectacles when you purport to have noted the mileage
readings both before and after Wise borrowed the van?"

"Correct."

"But I observed that you put them on to read the oath?"

"Yes, but I could have managed without."

"Of course the letters on the oath card are larger than the
figures on the milometer?"

"I agree."

"You'd have no objection to a small test of your eyesight?"
Mr. Milroy asked blandly while Mr. Gracey looked mystified.
"I have here"—he held up something which Mr. Colbourne had
just passed him—"a speedometer clock. I'd like you to look
at it without putting on your spectacles and tell the court what
the mileage reading is?"

An usher bore it across to Mr. Gracey, who received it as
enthusiastically as if it had been a grenade with the pin falling
out. Wise watched with malicious satisfaction as he held it
away from him and cocked his head in a squinting endeavour
to decipher the figures.

"Well?" Mr. Milroy prompted. The demonstration had
already proved his point and he didn't much care what answer
the witness gave.

"It looks like 6–9–0–6," Mr. Gracey said tentatively.

"Let me see it, please," the judge intervened. He turned to
Mr. Milroy. "I take it this is identical with the one fitted in the
witness's van?"

"Yes, my lord."

"The noughts and sixes are almost indistinguishable. Is it
6–9–0–0?"

161

"6–9–0–6, my lord," Mr. Milroy replied in a tone which bore a trace of faint discomfiture.

Wise bit his lip in annoyance and scribbled a note to Mr. Colbourne, who passed it on to Mr. Milroy, who read it and, turning to the witness, said, "You'd agree with me that there's rather more light where you're standing than there is in the interior of the van?"

Mr. Gracey shrugged. He was in no mood to make gracious concessions. "A bit more perhaps."

"You didn't find it particularly easy to read the figures, did you?"

"I got them right, didn't I?"

"Well, the jury will have observed your expression while you were examining the speedometer, and it's probably more a matter of comment, anyway," Mr. Milroy remarked quickly in an attempt to smother the effect of Mr. Gracey's minor triumph. He sat down and cast the jury a look of confidence.

P.C. Franklyn was the next witness. Mr. Brown led him through his evidence and, coming to his last question, asked, "Have you any doubt at all that the man you saw driving the Jaguar on that Saturday night was the accused?"

"None, sir."

"So little that you didn't dare run the risk of not picking him out on a properly conducted identification parade?" Mr. Milroy demanded as he was rising.

"Sir?" the officer said in nervous incomprehension.

"Wasn't that more comment than question?" the judge asked pleasantly.

"If your lordship pleases." Mr. Milroy looked severely at the witness. "What were the reports you took into Superintendent Manton's room when the accused was there?"

"I don't know, sir."

"Who gave them to you?"

"Detective-Sergeant Grant."

"Telling you to take them to the detective-superintendent?"

"Yes, sir."

"Do you often act as messenger boy for the C.I.D.?"

Franklyn blushed. "No, sir," he stammered.

"Had you ever done so before?"

"Yes, sir."

"When was the previous time?"

"I can't remember, sir."

"How many times since?"

The witness shook his head and looked uncomfortable. "I haven't kept a note, sir."

"Can you say why you were asked to do so on that occasion?"

"No, sir."

"I'll suggest the reason. You were told to go along to Superintendent Manton's room and see if you recognised the man there as the driver of the Jaguar. That's what happened, wasn't it?"

"No, sir."

"Are you quite sure?" Mr. Milroy asked in a quietly menacing tone.

"Yes, sir."

Franklyn was standing rigidly upright, staring straight ahead of him. His expression had become blank, and it was as though he had pulled down a shutter to protect him against Mr. Milroy's questions.

"Wise will say when he gives evidence that you took an unusual amount of interest in him when you entered the room. Stared at him closely. Is that correct?"

"No, sir."

Mr. Milroy leaned back against the row behind him and gave the witness an appraising stare.

"Look this way a moment, Franklyn." The officer complied. "Apart from his lordship, there are four other people sitting beside him on the bench. How many of them are wearing spectacles?"

There were several seconds of dramatic silence as all eyes turned expectantly on the witness, whose adam's apple bobbed furiously.

"I don't know, sir," he said at last in a strangled tone, and Mr. Milroy sat down with a triumphant look at the jury, saying as he did so, "Your powers of observation are apparently not as formidable today as they were that dark Saturday night."

"A most improper observation," Mr. Brown said, as he rose to restore his witness's evidence in re-examination.

But Mr. Milroy was unabashed by this and by the judge's unspoken displeasure. He had known his only chance of discrediting this particular facet of the prosecution's case was through the young constable, and that he would fail to dent either Manton or Sergeant Grant when they came to give evidence.

Wise was pleased to observe that the jury had appeared impressed by Mr. Milroy's virtuosity—save, that is, for the two males, who had continued, the one to look boorishly sceptical, the other arrogantly so.

The day came to an end and Colin Wise was taken back to Brixton. It seemed only a few minutes later that he was again standing halfway up the steps which led to the dock, waiting for the chief officer to motion him the rest of the way.

Witnesses came and went, with Mr. Milroy's cross-examination directed to casting doubt on the supposition that Goodwin was dead or that Wise could have had anything to do with his disappearance. Mr. Vallett of the laboratory repeated the evidence he had given before the magistrates and was questioned by Mr. Milroy to the same effect as he had been by Mr. Colbourne, though in greater detail. At the end of the line and late on the afternoon of the second day, Manton reached the witness-box. Mr. Milroy cross-examined him with restraint and did no more than make the formal suggestion that P.C. Franklyn's visit to his office had been prearranged, which Manton equally formally denied.

"But for that fortuitous circumstance," Mr. Milroy asked with faint sarcasm, "would you have put the accused up for identification?"

"Very probably, sir. But of course it didn't arise."

"Have you continued, even since the committal for trial, to try and find Goodwin?"

"We have, sir."

"Is it correct that you have never even found his passport or wallet?"

"It is, sir."

"So you really have no idea whether he is alive or dead?"

"I'm certain he is not alive, sir."

"What makes you say that in such a positive tone?"

"Because, if he had been, I'm sure our inquiries would have uncovered some trace or other."

"Have you not had previous experience of persons vanishing completely, only to turn up alive years later?"

"Yes, sir."

"Well then?"

"I'm only speaking about this case, sir, when I say I'm certain we'd have discovered if he were still alive."

"And you're basing that simply on the very full inquiries you have made and which have been the subject of a great deal of evidence?" The judge asked keenly.

"Yes, my lord."

Manton stepped down and Mr. Brown declared the prosecution's case to be closed. Mr. Colbourne had already conveyed Mr. Milroy's view to Wise that he thought it would be better tactics not to make a submission of no case to answer, which would probably fail here as it had in the magistrates' court, but immediately to call Wise into the witness-box.

"We'll adjourn until half-past ten tomorrow morning," Mr. Justice Raven announced as soon as Mr. Milroy had revealed the course he was taking.

There was the usual admonition to the jury not to allow anyone outside the court to discuss the case with them, and then after the exchange of ceremonial bows with which the day began and ended, the judge was gone and Wise was once more taken to the cells below to await the journey back to Brixton.

In the middle of the night he woke up and realised suddenly with startling clarity that the day which was about to break was likely to prove the most fateful of his life. In his mind's eye he saw clearly the faces of the twelve jurors, anonymous and unknown to each other, who had been plucked from nowhere to try him. He felt hideously frightened.

*　　　*　　　*　　　*　　　*

After an intense initial nervousness, Wise began rather to enjoy giving evidence. He realised, however, that it was better

165

to appear nervous than cocky, and it was with a certain amount of inner relish that he assumed what he reckoned to be the right blend of modesty and self-assurance.

Under Mr. Milroy's guidance he told how he had never known who his parents were, of his upbringing by the Pritchards and of his learning a trade and coming to London to seek work. Next Mr. Milroy asked him about his drawings, and he described how he would spend a happy Saturday or Sunday with his sketchbook, how he would visit the Tate and current exhibitions of modern art. He agreed with his counsel that it was his interest in art which had made him something more than a mere television repair man when he went to Goodwin's cottage, and went on to say how much he looked forward to and enjoyed his discussions with the vanished man.

"Mr. Goodwin was extremely kind to me and I greatly appreciated his interest in me," he said with just the right degree of sincerity.

After Mr. Milroy had questioned him about the fateful visit to Wise's flat, he asked, "Did you ever see or hear anything of Mr. Goodwin after that Friday evening?"

"No, sir."

"Have you any idea at all what happened to him?"

Wise shook his head. "None, sir," he replied in a firm tone.

"Were you the driver of his car on the Saturday night it was allegedly seen by P.C. Franklyn?"

"I have never driven Mr. Goodwin's car in my life, sir."

"Tell us what happened when you were in Superintendent Manton's office and Franklyn came in?"

"Well, sir, he brought in these papers and I didn't take much notice at first, but then I became aware that he was staring at me intently. It struck me as odd, but I still had no idea what it was all about. Nobody said anything, and indeed the next I knew was when he gave evidence in the other court."

After a few more questions Mr. Milroy sat down and Wise turned slightly to face Mr. Brown.

"You were reasonably well acquainted with Goodwin's habits,

weren't you, Wise?" The question was asked bluntly and in a tone which expected one answer only.

Not well enough or I wouldn't be here, was the reply which sprang to Wise's mind. Instead, however, he said quietly, "I don't think so, sir."

"You'd been to his home a good many times?"

"Eight or ten."

"And had all these discussions with him?"

"Yes," he replied warily.

"So that you knew quite a lot about him?"

"In what way?"

"What he liked and didn't like, what his tastes and interests were?"

"I didn't know everything about his likes and dislikes."

"I'm not suggesting you did, but you knew, for example, all about his intended trip to Australia?"

"Yes, sir, he'd told me."

"You knew he owned property out there?"

"Yes."

"And for how long he was going?"

"He told me six months."

"And how he was travelling?"

"Yes."

"And what was going to happen to his cottage while he was away?"

"I think he mentioned that Hilda would be keeping an eye on it."

"And the arrangements he'd made for his car?"

"Yes, I believe he mentioned that too."

"He told you a good deal about himself?" Wise shrugged helplessly and glanced toward Mr. Milroy. "Did he ever discuss his financial affairs with you?"

"No, never."

"Did you know he was a rich man?"

"He obviously had more money than I did," Wise replied with a faint smile, "but I didn't know how much he had. It was none of my business."

"Would you describe yourself as ambitious?"

"Moderately."

"You have expensive tastes?"

"It's not much good having them if you can't afford to indulge them, and I can't."

"Did Mr. Goodwin ever give you any presents?"

"He gave me a tip once or twice," Wise replied, with a puzzled expression.

"How much?"

"A pound or two."

"Nothing else?"

"No."

"Would you agree that you rather insinuated yourself into his life?"

Wise looked hurt. "No, sir, I wouldn't."

"Was he fond of you?"

"Fond? I think he liked me, but I wouldn't say he was fond of me."

"He liked you well enough to visit your home on the eve of a six-month absence from the country?"

"I've already explained why he came."

"And I'm suggesting that his visit indicated a rather stronger bond between you than you're admitting?"

"He came because he'd promised to see my drawings before he left," Wise replied with a note of faint exasperation.

"Who suggested that particular evening?"

"I did. I mean, it was the only convenient one."

"You knew it was his last?"

"Yes."

"I see," Mr. Brown observed in a silky tone. "Let me ask you something about his visit. He didn't mention any alteration in his plans for the next day?"

"No, sir."

"Or say where he was going when he left you?"

"I understood, home."

"His housekeeper has told the court he was worried he was starting a cold on Friday morning and that she noticed it. Did he mention that to you?"

"No, sir."

"Did you notice he had one?"

"I don't think so, sir," Wise replied with the note of caution creeping into his voice.

"Anyway, there was no suggestion of his not coming after all?"

"No, sir."

And so the questions continued to fall briskly from Mr. Brown, while Wise tried desperately to see beyond them in the split second before an answer was required. Once or twice he pulled back in time from a reply which could have given prosecuting counsel the lead in for which he was probing. Many of the questions seemed harmless, but Colin Wise never relaxed his guard. They went on for over an hour, by the end of which time he felt more tired than he ever had before. When at last he was allowed to return to the dock, he sat back exhausted to listen with one ear to Mr. Brown making his closing speech to the jury. He now realised that the pattern which prosecuting counsel had been intent on weaving by his cross-examination was one of a strange relationship in which there was more than the court had been told. He concluded by inviting the jury to say that the crown had proved its case.

Mr. Milroy, with greater vehemence and more emotional flashes, poured scorn on the points which Mr. Brown had commended to the jury's attention and told the twelve now rather distracted-looking jurors that there was only one possible verdict, namely, not guilty. "You have seen and heard Wise for yourselves," he concluded, "and I suggest that seldom in this court has a man accused of murder comported himself with such obvious honesty and integrity under a barrage of testing questions. Didn't his evidence leave you saying to yourselves, 'This man is innocent'?"

Mr. Justice Raven swivelled round in his chair to face the jury, who looked towards him as if he were their last hope of salvation in the sea of words which threatened to submerge them. Even the sour-faced juror turned with the rest, albeit reluctantly and with an expression which seemed to dare the judge to win him over.

In quiet, even tones, Mr. Justice Raven dealt first with the law. "Before the prisoner can be convicted of this charge," he told them, "the fact of death must have been proved to your satisfaction by the Crown by such circumstances as render the commission of the crime certain and leave no ground for reasonable doubt. The circumstantial evidence must be so cogent and compelling, members of the jury, as to convince you that on no rational hypothesis other than murder can the facts be accounted for. Let us now see what those facts are. . . ."

As Colin Wise listened he realised with a sudden leaping of his spirit that the judge was on his side. He was almost warning the jury against a conviction. Suspicion, however great, was never a substitute for evidence, he told them. On the other hand, the facts of the case were entirely a matter for their judgment and there were facts in this case which told both for and against the prisoner. It was for them, and them only, to decide where the truth lay. Were they satisfied the prosecution had discharged the burden of proof? Because, if not, then the accused was entitled to be acquitted.

By the time the end of his summing-up was reached, Wise half-expected the jury to return an immediate verdict without leaving the box, and it was with faint disappointment that he heard the judge give instructions that they should be allowed to take with them to the jury room any of the exhibits they wished.

Wise was hurried out of sight and locked in one of the cells below the court. This, he had heard several times since he'd been in Brixton, would be the worst part. *Allow 'em time to smoke at least one cigarette*, one or two old lags had said. *Don't expect 'em back in under half an hour in a murder case, it's the minimum time they reckon decent*, another had cautioned.

Accordingly for the first thirty minutes Wise sat back with eyes closed and tried to make his mind a blank. During the next thirty he began to fidget with his hands and wonder what the jury could be up to. It must be ten of them trying to make those two bastards see sense, but surely they couldn't hold out much longer against the persuasive powers of the majority? After a further half-hour, Wise imagined he could see the man with hair parted in the middle suddenly accept that he'd been misguided. Now they'd all turn on old sour-face and tell him not to be an

170

obstructionist. They'd cajole and if necessary threaten. Justice couldn't be thwarted by one man. *Come on*, they'd say, *it's time we returned to court. Everyone agreed, Not Guilty?* And old sour-face would grudgingly nod and look sourer than ever. . . .

In the fifth half-hour Wise was ready to scream. His nerve ends felt as if they'd been amputated with a rusty saw. From time to time one of the officers brought him cups of tea, which he compulsively gulped down.

And than a few minutes short of three hours the door was unlocked and he was taken dazed back into court. The jury filed into their seats looking punch-drunk and exhausted. Only his two enemies appeared unchanged. Finally, the judge came, wearing a faint air of displeasure.

He turned towards the jury and the foreman stood up.

"I understand," Mr. Justice Raven said tartly, "that you have been unable to agree upon a verdict?"

Wise closed his eyes and his head swam with despair. He forced them open and his ears to listen.

"That is so, my lord."

"I'm sure you appreciate how very desirable it is that you should reach a verdict if you possibly can. Desirable in the interest of the public as well as of the accused. Is there any further assistance I can give you?"

"I'm afraid not, my lord."

"Do you think if you retire again you might be able to come to a verdict?"

"No, my lord. There's no chance whatsoever of an agreement."

"Very well, I have no alternative but to discharge you and to order a re-trial at the next session of this court. In the meantime let all recognizances be enlarged."

It wasn't until he was back in Brixton Prison that night that Wise began to experience the full agony of his situation. He'd had almost more than he could take, and yet he had to go on. He mustn't surrender weakly now. After all, in one sense a fresh trial meant fresh hope.

18

One morning, about two and a half weeks later, Wise returned to the ward from exercise to find a newcomer in the bed next to his. He was a sharp-faced fellow with cruel eyes. He was sitting on his bed reading a newspaper as Wise came across.

"You Wise?" he asked in an aggressive tone, looking up from the newspaper he was reading.

"Yes."

"Seen this bit about you in the paper?"

"I haven't seen one today."

"Well, it's not, strictly speaking, about you," he went on in a voice Wise already found irritating. "They've dug up a bit of the body you're supposed to have done in." Wise stared at him in angry disbelief. "Here, read it yourself if you want." He thrust the paper towards Wise and stuck a begrimed finger over the paragraph. Wise turned his back on the man before bringing himself to read what was there. It ran:

"Goodwin Found?

"Mystery surrounds the finding yesterday afternoon of a severed leg in a wood not far from the cottage where author Geoffrey Goodwin lived. Police immediately sealed off the area and imposed a security ban. A spokesman later refused to confirm or deny that the limb had been found, but it is understood that the discovery was made by a twelve-year-old boy whose dog had dug it up. It will be recalled that the jury disagreed in the recent trial. . . . "

Wise let the paper drop on to his bed.

"Satisfied now?" The irritating voice demanded behind him.

"It doesn't say definitely that it's Mr. Goodwin's leg."

"You ought to know."

"I didn't kill him. I've always believed he was still alive."

172

It was the other man's turn to look incredulous. "Oh, I expect he is," he said with a rasping laugh. "Probably decided to cut off his leg and bury it before going to Australia. Expect he thought they liked pommies better that way."

Wise ignored him and went over to the centre table to look at another paper. Most of them carried the item on their front pages, and the only things which varied from one account to another was the degree of speculation.

That afternoon Mr. Colbourne came.

"You've seen the papers?" he asked, as soon as Wise was shown into the interview room where he was waiting.

"Yes. Is it definitely Mr. Goodwin's leg?"

"I gather there's no doubt at all. The foot has been identified by his chiropodist."

"Are the prosecution allowed to mention it at the re-trial?"

"Indeed they are—and will. They'll undoubtedly be serving a notice of additional evidence which'll comprise the statements of the lad whose dog dug it up, the pathologist who examined it and the chiropodist."

"Which leg was it?" Wise asked, as he tried to remember which way round he had buried them.

Mr. Colbourne gave him a curious look. "The right, I believe, but it doesn't make any difference. Whichever it is, the jury are not likely to have any difficulty now in concluding that Goodwin has been murdered."

"But that still doesn't make it me, sir."

"Even so, it immeasurably strengthens the prosecution's case and at the same time removes one of the main props of the defence."

Wise felt as if he was being strangled by Mr. Colbourne's remorseless logic. "But I'm still innocent," he declared in a desperate voice.

"And we'll continue to fight to get you acquitted," the solicitor said in a tone which carried little comfort for his client. "I'll be seeing Mr. Milroy in the next few days to discuss the latest developments. They'll serve a copy of the notice of additional evidence on you personally. Hang on to it; don't go and throw it down the pan as one of my clients once did."

Wise returned gloomily to the ward, then came to a sudden decision and sat down to write a letter. It was short and couched in careful terms though its purpose was plain. It solicited a visit from the recipient. When two days later Mr. Colbourne went to see Mr. Milroy at his chambers, he said to him, "The discovery of the leg has certainly shaken him, though he still insists that he is innocent."

"I don't wonder he's shaken," Mr. Milroy replied, "but it doesn't necessarily indicate his guilt. If he genuinely believed Goodwin was still alive, it must have come as a brutal shock."

"If," Mr. Trend said blandly.

A few days after this Mr. Colbourne received a request from Wise to see him again as he had something very important to tell his solicitor.

Mr. Colbourne came away from the prison deeply troubled.

*　　*　　*　　*　　*

As Colin Wise sat listening to Mr. Brown again opening the case for the prosecution, he felt like one of the cast in a long-running play. The atmosphere had become leaden and the leading actors were struggling against a sense of terrible ennui, even though there had been one major change of cast.

Mr. Justice Stuckey was one of the senior judges and was approximately twenty-five years older than Mr. Justice Raven. His wig was the colour of bean soup; his robe, though red, had none of the lustre of the previous judge's, and the ermine cuffs might have come from Aunt Emily's attic. And from where Wise sat his face appeared to be a congested mass of reds and purples. When he spoke, he gave the impression of dredging the words with difficulty from deep inside him.

On this occasion the jury was all-male. None of them looked hostile as had the two at the previous trial. On the other hand, they looked a better-educated lot and Wise was uncertain whether this would be in his favour or not. The foreman wore an old school tie and was very much a city gent.

"You will hear, members of the jury," Mr. Brown was saying, "that the leg which was the subject of this grisly discovery is indisputably the right leg of Geoffrey Goodwin, the deceased.

His chiropodist will tell you that he has no doubt of this, and you may feel inclined to accept his evidence on this point since he has attended to the dead man's feet for several years and has records showing the position of corns and callouses which are identical with those found on the foot attached to this leg. You will have, too, the evidence of Dr. Nourse, the pathologist, to the effect that this leg had been crudely severed from the trunk after death." He rested both hands on the ledge in front of him, and, bending forward, said with great earnestness, "You will probably agree, members of the jury, that much of the evidence I have outlined to you assumes a new significance in the light of the discovery of this limb. The marks in the bath, for example; the borrowing of Mr. Gracey's van and the scrubbing out it received the next day; the lies about the mileage. Don't they all indicate quite clearly that the deceased met his death in the prisoner's flat—I can't tell you how, but surely violently—that his body was dismembered in the bath and then conveyed in Mr. Gracey's van for interment about the countryside. One leg, the right leg of this unfortunate man, has come to light, but can you doubt that other portions of his body lie hidden and awaiting discovery? Perhaps they never will be found, but from your point of view in trying this case, does it matter very much?"

And so once more the witnesses began their traffic to and from the witness-box, and Mr. Brown and Mr. Milroy took their turns in the bombardment of questions. This time, however, Mr. Milroy could not spring his surprise of the speedometer clock on Mr. Gracey, nor put P.C. Franklyn's identification to the same ingenious test. Indeed, no sooner had this officer taken the oath than he could be seen overtly memorising every detail of the scene within his gaze. When Mr. Gracey had come into court he'd cast Wise a look of bitter resentment. Wise knew that he had hurt him and was glad.

The additional witnesses gave their evidence and were not cross-examined. Wise had gathered that his counsel saw no purpose in attacking evidence which was almost unassailable since it didn't take the prosecution's case any further in proving that Wise was the murderer. Mr. Milroy did, however, go further in his efforts to discredit Mr. Vallett's evidence about the marks in the bath and secured an admission from this witness that it was perhaps more likely than he had previously conceded that they could have been caused in an attempt at removing paint.

Owing to the additional witnesses and to the constant plaintive and petulant objections of Mr. Justice Stuckey that he must be allowed time to take proper note of the evidence, it was mid-morning on the third day before Wise returned to the witness-box.

His evidence under examination-in-chief was no different from what it had been the first time, save that Mr. Milroy's questions led him into greater detail in rebutting the suggestion that Goodwin had been cut up in the bath and that Mr. Gracey's van had been used as a hearse.

Mr. Brown's cross-examination traversed the same ground as before and with the same result. It had to be re-enacted for the benefit of the new jury, Wise supposed, as he firmly parried the well-worn questions. Suddenly, however, Mr. Brown asked: "Having heard all the evidence, Wise, are you still saying that you are the innocent victim of circumstances?"

"I must be, since I didn't kill Mr. Goodwin. I had no motive to do so."

"Did you ever hear Mr. Goodwin refer to someone named Peter Fox?"

Wise frowned as though in thought. How far was prosecuting counsel going along this tack? "No, I don't remember the name," he said slowly.

"Do you know anyone of that name?"

He shook his head. "No."

"Doesn't Mr. Gracey have a customer called Fox?"

"The old blind man, do you mean?"

"Yes, so you do know who I mean?"

"Yes."

"Why then did you first deny knowing anyone of that name?"

"I wasn't thinking about old Mr. Fox. I didn't know him well. I've only met him once or twice when I've been to his house to repair his radio."

"Have you ever visited him socially?"

"Never." He knew that his answers were safe, since the prosecution would clearly have called Patrick Fox as a witness if they had obtained any information from him.

As Wise returned to the dock, he heard Mr. Milroy utter the words for which he had been impatiently waiting throughout the three days.

"I call Miss Lesley Gracey."

Lesley's arrival in the witness-box would have satisfied any film star. Mr. Brown watched her take the oath with an expression of wary surprise and then leant forward to hold a whispered conversation with the D.P.P.'s representative. The jury cast each other uneasy sidelong glances and even the judge looked puzzled. Here indeed was the surprise witness whom no one had expected. Colin Wise gazed at her with quiet satisfaction. In one gesture he was helping himself and scoring off his late employer. Mr. Colbourne had been dubious, even hostile to the idea, but he had insisted, and after all it was, as he had firmly pointed out, *his* liberty which was at stake. And he would almost say that it had been worth it just to see her father's expression when she came into the witness-box. God, he had looked bitter, but there was nothing he had been able to do in the face of his daughter receiving a subpoena.

With a gratifying degree of composure Lesley answered Mr. Milroy's opening questions.

"I want to come now," he said, "to the Friday evening, that is the evening of the alleged murder." Lesley nodded intently. "Where did you spend that evening?"

"At Colin's flat."

"What time did you arrive there?"

"About half-past eight."

"Was anybody else there at the same time as yourself?"

"Someone was leaving as I arrived."

"Who was that?"

"Colin told me it was Mr. Goodwin."

"I should have asked you this before, Miss Gracey. Was Wise expecting you?"

She smiled shyly. "No. I just dropped in." She's almost as smooth a liar as I am, Wise reflected.

"Did you notice a car parked outside?"

"Yes, a grey Jaguar."

"And whereabouts did you pass Mr. Goodwin?"

"He was just coming out of the gate. I saw him get into the car and drive away."

"And how long did you stay in Wise's company?"

"About two hours."

"And then?"

"He drove me home."

"In what?"

"My father's van, which he had borrowed."

"And during the time you were with him, did Mr. Goodwin ever return?"

"No."

"Did Wise say he was expecting him back?"

"No, he said he was leaving for Australia the next day."

"Did you happen to go into the bathroom while you were at Wise's flat?"

"Yes."

"What did you notice?"

"Some marks in the bath."

"And that was after you had seen Goodwin leave alive and well?"

"Yes."

"Thank you, Miss Gracey."

Mr. Brown, who had been having a hurried conversation with Manton, rose to his feet.

"Are you fond of Wise?"

"Yes."

"Very fond of him?"

She nodded vigorously.

"Would you do anything you could to help him?"

"Yes, but what I've said is the truth."

"Is it true that your father didn't approve of your seeing Wise?"

"He still treats me like a baby," she replied defiantly.

"Why didn't you come forward and give this evidence at the first trial?"

"Colin wanted to save me if he possibly could. He was thinking of me."

"You mean, he thought he had a strong enough defence without calling on you?"

"Yes. He said he would only ask me to come to court as a last resort."

Mr. Brown pulled his gown higher on to his shoulders. "Had you ever seen Mr. Goodwin before?"

"No."

"Describe him." Lesley's jaw dropped and her face seemed to fall apart. "Go on, describe him," Mr. Brown urged.

Wise closed his eyes in a sudden sinking agony. Why had she wanted to testify she'd passed him as he came out of the gate. He'd told her to say she'd seen the car pulling away as she came down the road. A grey Jaguar was all she'd had to remember. He opened his eyes and stared at her, urgently trying to telepathise Goodwin's description across the twenty unbridgeable feet which separated dock from witness box.

"Was he wearing a hat?" Mr Brown went on, closing in for the kill. "A coat?" He paused and then said quite quietly, "You never saw him at all, did you? You never went to Wise's flat that night, did you? . . . Did you?"

Lesley began to tremble, her eyes searched vainly for succour amongst the sea of faces around her, and then with a terrible sob she lurched sideways over the edge of the witness-box.

For a few seconds there was pandemonium, which Wise surveyed with searing fury. He heard Mr. Milroy say in a stiff, formal voice, "That is the case for the defence, my lord."

There followed speeches and summing-up, which Wise hardly heard, though they occupied the remainder of the day. Indeed the judge didn't complete his summing-up until the next morning. The jury were out for an hour and ten minutes before returning a verdict of guilty.

"The sentence of the court is that you be imprisoned for life," Mr. Justice Stuckey pronounced in his out-of-breath tones.

Mr. Colbourne visited Wise in the cells before he was taken to Wormwood Scrubs. Brixton Prison had seen the last of him.

"I want to appeal," he said.

"We first have to find grounds."

"That's easy," he remarked bitterly, "on the grounds that I'm innocent."

"We can only appeal on a point of law."

"Well, there must be something."

"I'll be seeing Mr. Milroy after we've received a copy of the transcript. Meanwhile you can certainly apply for leave to appeal." Mr. Colbourne looked embarrassed. "I'm sorry about Miss Gracey, but I did——" He caught sight of Wise's expression and broke off. As he said later to his wife, "If looks could kill I'd be dead by now. I believe he's mad. I never liked the idea of calling that girl. I told him the jury were bound to wonder why she hadn't given evidence at the first trial."

"But you thought she was telling the truth, dear. You told me so."

"I'm sure I never said that. The truth of her evidence was always for the jury to decide. What I may have said was that she made quite a favourable impression on me when she came to the office and that I accepted as plausible her explanation—his, too—as to why she hadn't come forward before. I think the thing which clinched it for me was his reminding me that before the first trial he had asked me whether a witness might help his case."

"You don't still think he's innocent, do you, dear?" Mrs. Colbourne asked anxiously.

"The jury's answered that question," he replied firmly, then sighed. "No, I don't, but I wish I knew something about why he did it, if he did do it. He must have done it."

"Have a drink?" his wife suggested.

Mr. Colbourne fetched himself a glass of sherry. "Oh well, now for the appeal and then it'll be all over."

Two weeks later Wise made the journey to the Law Courts where the Court of Criminal Appeal sat. He found himself sitting rather like anonymous royalty in a discreetly curtained box which provided him with an oblique view of the proceedings. Three red-robed judges sat sideways on to him facing counsel. There were the familiar faces of Mr. Milroy and Mr. Trend separated by a narrow gangway from Mr. Brown. Mr. Colbourne sat at a large table in front of Mr. Milroy. He gave Wise a glance of non-recognition as he was ushered into his box, but otherwise kept his eyes fixed on the three judges. He had been to see Wise twice in Wormwood Scrubs and each time had seemed more withdrawn and monosyllabically fatalistic.

For an hour and forty minutes Mr. Milroy argued that Mr. Justice Stuckey had misdirected the jury in a number of vital respects, but it was clear from the start, even to Wise himself, that he was making no impression on the court. At least not the desired one. He was finally halted by a blizzard of interruptions from the three judges and sat down.

"We needn't call on you, Mr. Brown," the judge in the centre announced, and then proceeded in short sharp sentences to announce that Mr. Justice Stuckey had conducted the proceedings with his customary skill and fairness and that the appeal would be dismissed.

Back in prison, Wise fumed and chafed for a while. He wrote petitions to the Home Secretary and even managed to get letters smuggled out to his M.P. and to the editor of a national newspaper which was known for championing lone causes if they had sufficient publicity value. In all of these he protested his innocence and wrongful conviction. Indeed, he had already been encouraged by a certain element of public disquiet which his case had occasioned. Nobody actually said the jury's verdict was wrong, but it had become general to emphasise the unexplained mysteries which still surrounded the case. If Wise could foster doubt, then at least, he reckoned, he would stand every chance of an earlier release.

One evening, not long after the dismissal of the appeal, Manton happened to run into Mr. Colbourne and they began to discuss the case.

"Frankly," Manton said, "I thought he'd got away with it. The first time, that is, before we'd found part of the body."

"Did you ever learn why the jury disagreed?"

."My little bird told me they were initially split straight down the middle. Six for a conviction, six for an acquittal. And that the final count was eight to convict and four to acquit. A couple of waverers had been won over, apparently. I gather," he added with an impish grin, "that none of them doubted Franklyn was telling the truth, so the four must have had other grounds for wishing to acquit. With juries, you just don't know. . . ."

"Any idea who the four were?"

"Both the women and I don't know whether you noticed a pretty disagreeable-looking chap with a red face. He was one and I don't know who the fourth was." Manton chuckled. "The red-faced man, I later found out, had had a recent brush with the law himself. False pretences or something. Even though he'd got off, he was still smarting."

"Interesting," Mr. Colbourne remarked drily. "Any views about motive?"

"I thought that was going to be our undoing. Not being able to prove one, I mean. Personally, I'm sure he somehow got hold of that six thousand pounds which we've never been able to trace beyond the shadowy Peter Fox. He covered his tracks too well, but my bet is that he has that nicely salted away. He's a clever boy, Colin Wise, even if not quite as clever as he'd hoped."

And this curiously had become the theme of Wise's own thinking as he gradually settled down to prison life. Even though he hadn't got away with the whole stupendous plan— and it was the purest piece of bad luck which had been his undoing—he still had the six thousand pounds to look forward to when he came out, and if he played his cards sensibly he should still be under thirty when that day arrived. Alone he had out-witted them. They had never even got round to detecting the cheque as a forgery. No, he'd been clever all right, and, what was more important, he had learnt from his mistakes and would know how to profit by them when he was released. Profit—yes, that was the word. He'd begin planning right away.

Mr. J. Hillard, the clerk in the Earls Court branch of the Southern Bank who had received six thousand pounds over the counter for the credit of Mr. William Carter's account—had followed the Wise case with considerable interest. He had at quite an early stage recognised Wise as Carter from the photographs which had appeared in the newspapers. It took him a little longer to realise, however, that he and Wise were probably the only two people in the world to know who William Carter was.

He had felt no loyalty towards his employers ever since he had been passed over for promotion, and very little before which was the main reason for their neglect of him.

At about the same time as Colin Wise was beginning to give thought to his future, the clerk handed in his notice, which was received without regret, and walked out of the bank for the last time six thousand pounds richer.

It had been a simple matter to close Mr. Carter's account and spirit the funds away. Simpler by far for him than it had been for Wise to juggle with it.

As he caught a bus home that evening, he decided what his first purchase would be—a nice family saloon in which he would be able to take his placid wife and two demanding children for trips to the seaside.

He had never wanted to possess a Rolls Royce or one of those three-thousand-pound gleaming sports jobs, but a good sensible car of popular make such as everyone save millionaires, spivs and crooks aspired to own.

He couldn't wait to break the news to his family of new treats in store, and in so far as he spared a thought for Colin Wise it was to hope that in his case *life* would mean *life*.

››› If you've enjoyed this book and would like to discover more great vintage crime and thriller titles, as well as the most exciting crime and thriller authors writing today, visit: ›››

The Murder Room
Where Criminal Minds Meet

themurderroom.com